ABBY
IN BETWEEN
READY OR NOT!

BY **MEGAN E. BRYANT**

Penguin Workshop

W

PENGUIN WORKSHOP
An imprint of Penguin Random House LLC, New York

First published in the United States of America by Penguin Workshop,
an imprint of Penguin Random House LLC, New York, 2022

Text copyright © 2022 by Megan E. Bryant
Illustrations copyright © 2022 by Penguin Random House LLC

Illustrations by Christina Forshay

Penguin supports copyright. Copyright fuels creativity, encourages diverse voices,
promotes free speech, and creates a vibrant culture. Thank you for buying an
authorized edition of this book and for complying with copyright laws by not
reproducing, scanning, or distributing any part of it in any form without permission.
You are supporting writers and allowing Penguin to continue
to publish books for every reader.

PENGUIN is a registered trademark and PENGUIN WORKSHOP
is a trademark of Penguin Books Ltd, and the W colophon
is a registered trademark of Penguin Random House LLC.

Visit us online at penguinrandomhouse.com.

Library of Congress Cataloging-in-Publication Data is available.

Printed in the United States of America

ISBN 9780593226520   10 9 8 7 6 5 4 3 2 1 LSCC

This book is a work of fiction. Any references to historical events, real people,
or real places are used fictitiously. Other names, characters, places,
and events are products of the author's imagination, and any resemblance
to actual events or places or persons, living or dead, is entirely coincidental.

The publisher does not have any control over and does not assume any
responsibility for author or third-party websites or their content.

Design by Mary Claire Cruz

FOR CLARA,
WHO HELPED ME REMEMBER
AND INSPIRED THIS BOOK.
I LOVE YOU.

CHAPTER 1

At Zoe's house there weren't a lot of rules, except bigger is better, and brighter is best. So when Zoe invited me over to decorate cupcakes, I knew it was going to be incredible. Beyond incredible, even—*astounding*. There were, like, a *hundred* vanilla-and-strawberry-swirl cupcakes. And the toppings? You would not believe. Sprinkles, all mixed up in a rainbow jumble. Sparkly sugar in every color. Tiny, shiny gold stars. Candy confetti. Shimmery sugar pearls. A bowl of rock candy glinting like jewels. And there were bags of frosting and a bunch of pointed metal tips for piping flowers and leaves and squiggles.

Zoe looked up from a piece of waxed paper covered with frosting doodles. "Abby! Check it out," she said. "I've been practicing."

"Cool," I replied. Zoe is my cousin and my best friend forever, and not necessarily in that order. She's awesome in all the best ways: smart and fun and silly and nice. Together, we are A to Z and everything in between.

"How do you use this thing, anyway?" I asked, grabbing a pastry bag filled with sky-blue frosting. I tried holding it like a pencil. Drawing is my thing; it's what I do better than anything else, but I could tell right away that the pastry bag was not going to work like one of my art supplies.

"Here, I'll show you," Zoe said, sounding important. Teaching me stuff was probably her thing—after gymnastics and mythology and baking—and I didn't mind one bit. She was only a year older than me, but somehow Zoe knew way more about almost everything.

Take decorating cupcakes. From leaves to rose petals to swirly whirls, Zoe's designs were just right, and after a little practice, mine weren't too bad. We decorated every single one of those cupcakes with loopy swoops of buttercream frosting and then covered them in sparkly, sugary toppings.

Zoe got one of those secret-y smiles on her face—the kind that made me sit up a little straighter, knowing she was about to do something surprising.

"Check this out," she said as she dabbed a dollop of frosting on each one of her perfectly polished fingernails. Then she stuck her hands into the sprinkles!

"Zoe!" I screeched.

"Shhh!" She shushed me. Then she held up her hands. The sprinkles had stuck to the frosting on her nails like a confetti manicure.

"Ta-da!" Zoe announced, wiggling her fingers at me. A couple sprinkles fell off and bounced around the tablecloth, but Zoe didn't care.

"Wow," I said, impressed like always.

Zoe popped her index finger into her mouth. "Yum," she said. "Your turn!"

I picked up the bag and squeezed some of the frosting onto my nails. It wasn't as easy as Zoe made it look, but she cheered me on until I had a sprinkles manicure, too. By the end of it, we were laughing so hard that sprinkles were sproinging everywhere, and I just knew we'd have to get out the vacuum to clean up the mess, but I didn't even care. Everything was perfect.

Well, almost perfect.

The only thing in the whole wide world that could've

made it truly perfect was if we didn't need the cupcakes at all. Because those cupcakes were for Zoe's goodbye party. Zoe and her family were moving all the way from North Carolina to California, and I couldn't begin to imagine what life was going to be like without her.

* * *

Later that day, I spent most of Zoe's goodbye party staring at her shoes. They were basically the best shoes ever: rainbow, streaked with glitter, slip-ons. Half sneaker, half party shoe, they would go with *anything*. I could wear them *anywhere*.

If they were mine, I mean, and not Zoe's.

Plus, they twinkled and sparkled whenever she moved, so you couldn't *not* look at them.

That wasn't the real reason why I couldn't stop staring at those amazing shoes, though. To be totally honest, it was easier to look down than up. Looking up meant seeing Zoe's face and missing it already, even though she was sitting right next to me. Looking up meant people might see the tears that kept sneaking into my eyes. I didn't want to be mad at Uncle Craig about his new job, but if he'd found a job here in North Carolina instead of California, none of this would be happening.

Goodbye parties, I decided, were dumber than dumb. They just didn't make sense. Parties are supposed to be happy times, and goodbyes are sad, unless you are saying goodbye to the flu or the last bite of kale salad on your plate.

Then Aunt Rachel appeared. She was carrying a small box wrapped in gold paper. "We were going to give this to you later, Zoe," Aunt Rachel began. "But . . . since everyone is here now . . ."

Zoe's glittery purple nails flashed as she sloooowly peeled the tape off the present. At last, the paper slipped off and fluttered to the ground.

Zoe gasped.

I gasped.

Everybody gasped.

Inside the box was a phone. A cell phone. Zoe's first cell phone.

"Mooooommmmmmm!" Zoe shrieked. "Seriously? Are you serious?"

"So serious," Aunt Rachel said, beaming. "We want you to stay in touch with all your friends after the move. And since just about everybody is here, you can get their contact information!"

"I've already downloaded a bunch of apps," Uncle Craig said. "Messaging apps and photo apps and research apps and, yes, games . . ."

"Thank you!" Zoe was saying, but now she was the one who wouldn't look up. I couldn't blame her. The glow from Zoe's new phone lit up her whole face.

All around me, Zoe's friends from gymnastics were getting out *their* phones. At the same time—

Bing!

Zzzzz!

Dee-dee-dee!

WOOF!

Everyone laughed as their phones beeped and buzzed and woofed. I guess they were texting each other or something. If I had a phone, I could sit with them and text and laugh, too.

Suddenly, I realized I was the *only* one who didn't have a phone. Nobody seemed to notice that fact, so I figured nobody would notice if I slipped away from the group. And I was right! They didn't.

There was a table by the front door where everyone had put little presents for Zoe. My present was a stationery set, which is fancy paper for writing letters. The purple paper had purple flamingos on it, because flamingos are our favorite, thanks to Mrs. Flamingo. That's not her real name—at least, I don't think it is—but it's what we call her because she has a flock of plastic flamingos in her front yard that she dresses up every holiday. Mrs. Flamingo doesn't know it, but her flamingos are the whole reason I got really into art. Back when I was in second grade, I wanted to draw her flamingos, but every time I tried, they looked like pink potatoes with legs. Mom signed me up for art classes, and in less than a year, I was good enough at drawing that my flamingo picture won third prize at the county fair. Anyway, I just knew that whenever Zoe used her new stationery, she'd think of me and remember all the laughs we had about Mrs. Flamingo's flock.

The best part, though, was that I had matching stationery at my house. Blue paper with blue flamingos on it. It was going to be so great because Zoe and I could write each other letters on our flamingo paper, and those flamingos would fly back and forth across the country, landing in our mailboxes.

I walked into the dining room, and that's when I saw trouble. My brother, Max, had also wandered away from the party. This was a big problem because he was only four years old. And it was an even bigger problem because Aunt Rachel had left those fancy cupcake displays pretty close to the edge of the dining room table.

Max, of course, had found them.

He'd climbed one of the chairs and was leaning so far forward onto the table that he was practically lying on it. And he was doing something with the cupcakes. Not just something—he was messing with them. He was messing with Zoe's special goodbye party cupcakes!

"Max!" I said, trying to sound like Mom when she whisper-yells. "What are you doing?"

Max didn't stop. He didn't even bother to look at me. I stepped into the room with my hands on my hips and my eyes squinched into a mean squint.

That's when I realized that Max was picking sprinkles off the cupcakes! He had made six different color-coded piles right there on the tablecloth.

"Ewww! Are you touching all the cupcakes with your gross, dirty hands?" I asked.

"No," he said. "I'm not touching the cupcakes. I'm just touching the sprinkles."

"Why?" I demanded.

"I'm getting the red ones," he said. "Red ones taste best. Like cherries and strawberries."

"They do not," I told him. "Sprinkles all taste the same. It doesn't matter what color they are."

"Bzzzzz! Wrong!" Max announced. Ever since he'd seen a game show on TV, he liked pretending to be a buzzer. "I want my cupcake to be all red sprinkles."

Reasoning with Max is basically impossible, but I tried, anyway. "Look," I said. "Even *if* they tasted different, you know it's wrong to do this to all the cupcakes, right? They don't belong to you. It's selfish to take all the red sprinkles for yourself."

Max pretended he didn't hear me as he went back to picking more sprinkles off the cupcakes. Things were getting desperate. Then I had an idea.

"You know Zoe's opening presents now, right?" I asked. "And you're missing it?"

Max's head snapped back, and his eyes went wide. He hates the idea of missing out more than anything. Don't even show him pictures from before he was born. He'll be mad for the rest of the day that he wasn't there.

"Go!" I said, giving him a little push. "Quick! Before she finishes!"

Max scrambled out of the room, thankfully, and I tried to sneak the sprinkles back onto the cupcakes. That was not an easy thing to do. It turned out that sprinkles don't want to stick to frosting that's already set. I guess you just get one chance with sprinkles.

"Ratzit," I muttered as the sprinkles sproinged and boinged off the cupcakes and back onto the table. *Ratzit* is a word I made up, for when stuff is extra frustrating or annoying. It's like a swear word but even better, because you don't get in trouble for saying it.

"Uh-oh," a voice behind me said. "What's wrong?"

I spun around to see Zoe standing in the doorway. Double ratzit! She was going to see the sprinkle disaster before I had figured out how to fix it.

"I'm sorry, Z," I said, gesturing to the sprinkle piles. "It was Max. He had this dumb idea that each color has its own flavor."

I was worried Zoe would be mad, but instead, she tilted her head to the side and asked, "Do they?"

I shrugged. "I don't know."

"Let's find out," she said.

Then—I am not even kidding—Zoe licked her thumb, stuck it into the pile of purple sprinkles, and popped them into her mouth!

"Well?" I asked.

"Very unique flavor," she said. "Kind of a cross between grapes and blueberry pancakes and . . ."

"And?"

"Balloons!" she said, giggling.

I started laughing, too, as I tossed a bunch of yellow sprinkles into my mouth. "Mmm. Lemon, for sure," I said. "And daffodils and . . . raincoats!"

"Raincoats?" Zoe asked. She started really cracking up, and soon, we were both laughing so hard that when we tried to sample the sprinkles, we ended up spitting them out instead. Now the tears in my eyes were from laughing, but I still had that hollow, hurting place right in my middle. There was so much I wanted to say: *Don't leave* and *I'm going to miss you more than anything* and *Who will laugh with me like this after you move?*

I squashed all that down, though, and said, "Your new phone is so awesome. I wish I had one."

"Tell your mom you need one," Zoe said, like she understood what I really meant. "Not want. *Need*. How am I going to survive California if we can't talk every day?"

"Oh, come on." I sighed. "It's going to be amazing. Summer all the time, your own swimming pool . . ."

"No snow day sleepovers, no leaf piles, no flamingo house," Zoe said, ticking them off on her fingers. "No you."

I tried to smile, but it was wobbly.

"That's why you need a phone," Zoe continued. "We can text all the time and send each other pictures and memes. It will be like nothing has changed!"

"You think?" I asked slowly.

"I promise," she said.

That settled it. Zoe never made promises unless she really, truly meant it.

Now all I had to do was convince Mom and Dad to get me a phone.

❀   ❀   ❀

I couldn't wait for the party to end so I could talk to Mom and Dad. Maybe we could go buy a phone tonight! We stepped outside into the muggy, sticky August evening to walk exactly two blocks home. I knew I had to ask right away, before Max started on one of his endless, pointless stories about his favorite show. I was so eager that we weren't even halfway down Zoe's front path when I asked them straight-out, no warm-up or anything. That was a mistake.

"Sorry," Mom said, shaking her head. "It's just too soon."

"We've talked about this, Abby," Dad said.

"I know," I said. "It's just . . . Zoe's leaving, and I'm going to miss her so much—"

"That's why we ordered matching stationery for you two," Mom reminded me. I hated when she did that—interrupting like she knew what I was going to say before I even said it.

"But wait," I said. "What about *Zoe*?"

"*You* need a phone for Zoe?" Mom asked. Then she and Dad smiled at each other, like I was a little kid who wouldn't notice.

"Everyone acts like the move is bad for only me," I pushed on. "But what about her? She said she's going to miss me so much, and it would make it so much easier if she could talk to me every day! And how can she talk to me every day if I don't have my own phone?"

Mom sighed. "I know it's really hard to wait for something you want so much," she began. "And I wish that Aunt Rachel hadn't done that with the phone for Zoe—making a big scene of it in front of everyone."

"She and Uncle Craig feel terrible about the move," Dad added. "They know they're turning Zoe's whole life upside down."

"But we just feel like nine years old is too young to have a cell phone," Mom finished. "I'm sorry, Abby."

"So . . . when I'm ten?" I asked hopefully. Ten was not too far away—just five months. And everybody knew that double digits was a *big* deal.

But Mom shook her head again. "Sorry, sweet pea," she repeated. "I signed a pledge online. It's called 'Wait Until Eighth.'"

This was news to me.

"Wait until *what*?" I asked.

"Wait Until Eighth," Mom said. "Eighth grade. There's research that shows—"

"Eighth grade?" I howled. "Are you serious? You can't be serious! That's four years away!"

"The research—" Mom tried again.

"But what about Zoe? She can't talk to me for four years?"

"Oh, Abby, don't be so dramatic," Mom said. "Of course she can talk to you, on my phone or Daddy's phone."

"That's not the same! You know that's not the same!" I exclaimed. "I can't believe you're doing this to us because of some stupid pledge!"

"Hey now," Mom said, frowning.

"It *is* a stupid pledge," I insisted. "It doesn't even rhyme right. It should be, like, *waith* until *eighth*, which makes more sense, and by *more*, I mean *none*."

Dad snort-laughed and tried to cover it with a cough, but that just made Mom madder.

"You're out of line," she told me. "That's not the tone of voice you use when you speak to your parents."

"Well, maybe my parents shouldn't go around signing stupid online pledges that affect my whole life without even talking to me first," I shot back.

I was so mad that I tripped on our front step, like I hadn't walked up it a thousand times before. Dad's hand rested on my shoulder to steady me. His hand was warm and strong, and made some of my anger melt away. That was no good because it left me feeling all empty again.

"Why don't you take five in your room, princess," he said in a low voice near my ear.

"Don't call me 'princess' anymore," I said. "I don't like it."

If Dad was surprised by how rude I was being, he didn't show it. "Okay, I won't," he said. "I'll just have to think up a new nickname for you."

I glanced over at Mom to see how upset she was. It was impossible to tell because she was already walking inside, staring at her phone, like the discussion was over, like all my feelings and opinions didn't matter.

Like *I* didn't matter.

Well, at least I was mad again.

"Fine," I said in a very not-fine! voice, and stomped down the hallway. I slammed my bedroom door, but only a little loud. I didn't want to get in more trouble.

I flopped facedown on my bed with a big sigh.

And that's when I felt them.

Two bumps, right on my chest.

Where did they come from? I swear they weren't there when I woke up this morning.

Or were they?

Everything else whooshed out of my head as I poked, just a little, at one of the bumps. Yup. It was definitely there, no matter how much I wanted to pretend it wasn't.

Just what I need, I thought. *One* more *thing to worry about!*

CHAPTER
2

When I woke up the next morning, the bumps were still there. It wasn't a dream, and maybe that's good, because that would be a very weird dream. Then again, if it was a dream, I could laugh and forget about it. Dream bumps were nothing to worry about.

Real bumps, though? That definitely seemed worry-worthy.

I jumped out of bed, turned on the light, and stood in front of the mirror over my dresser. Then I pulled off my T-shirt and stared at my reflection. I looked the same as always. And by that I mean my chest was super flat. If I couldn't see the bumps, then nobody else could see them, either.

But I could feel them. They were definitely there, right under my nipples, like hard little marbles hiding under my skin. I poked my chest again, just to be sure.

Yup. Marble-bumps. They were feeling a little sore, too, and that made me start worrying even more. Were they sore last night? Were they sore because they were something *bad*?

Or were they sore because I kept poking them? To be honest, I'd been poking them kind of a lot.

What if they weren't bumps at all, but *lumps*? Last year, Aunt Rachel had a *lump*, and all the grown-ups acted super serious and worried and tried to hide it from Zoe and me. But we weren't as clueless as they thought. When Aunt Rachel's lump turned out to be nothing serious, she was so happy, she cried.

What was the difference between a bump and a lump, anyway?

Mom would know. I'd have to tell Mom. Maybe even show her.

I peeked at the clock. It was still pretty early. Maybe I could tell her before breakfast, and she'd reassure me that everything was fine and tell me not to worry so much. Yes. She was probably getting dressed. I'd go to her room—

Wham!

My bedroom door flew open so hard, it hit the wall, and there was Max, standing in the doorway like it was no big deal. Like he hadn't just barged in on me, half naked, poking my bump-lumps.

"Get out!" I shrieked in my shriekiest voice. My arm flew up to my chest to cover—what? It's not like there was anything to see. But I did it anyway.

Max just stood there, staring at me like I was a sea monster or something. "What are you doing?" he asked.

"GET OUT!" I shrieked again. "You didn't even *knock!*"

Max didn't move for a loooong moment. Then he stepped backward, closed the door, and knocked.

"Go away," I yelled through the door.

"But I knocked!" he yelled back.

"I want you to leave me alone!" I said. "I'm getting dressed!"

Yeah, that was a good excuse, in case Max told anyone what he saw. I was just getting dressed, not staring at my bare chest in the mirror like a weirdo.

There was a long pause. I had a feeling Max was still in the hallway. He's really good at lurking. Finally, his voice piped up again. "Mom says breakfast is ready, and it's special so you should come eat already."

Ratzit. I guess I missed my chance to talk to Mom privately before breakfast.

"Are you coming?" Max asked.

"I. Am. Getting. Dressed," I said through the door. "I'll come when I'm ready!"

Silence. Then I heard Max, bumping and banging down the hall. He was all over the place. But at least he was gone.

Well. I couldn't spend the whole day staring at myself in the mirror. And now I really did have to get dressed, and fast.

Downstairs, Mom was opening take-out containers from our favorite restaurant, The Breakfast Place. She always remembers everybody's favorite everything, so there was an omelet full of veggies and cheese for Dad. Max had a waffle with whipped cream and strawberry syrup, and my box had a giant stack of blueberry pancakes. And there was a box from Dizzy's Donuts. *And* a platter of bagels, even the rainbow ones she never buys because food coloring is chemicals.

First, I was really excited about the doughnuts. But then I narrowed my eyes as I stared at the feast. Mom must have gotten up at dawn to pick up all this food. It wasn't anybody's birthday.

So what was going on?

Does she know about my bumps? I wondered. Impossible! Or . . . maybe not. Sometimes Mom just, like, *knows* stuff. Like when I hid a bag of chocolate chips under my bed so I could have a private chocolate party whenever I wanted, or when Max tried to turn the bathtub into an aquarium. It's like she has the world's most annoying superpower.

I crossed my arms over my chest. If Mom was going to have a big breakfast celebration over my bumps, I would deny everything!

"Good morning, everybody!" Mom sang out. Her voice seemed brighter and louder than usual. She looked over at Dad, who nodded encouragingly at her.

"I . . . have some big news," Mom continued. "I'm . . . going back to work!"

Nobody said anything. I mean, what could we say? This was an even bigger surprise than my bumps.

"I interviewed for a paralegal job at the firm of Taylor, Taylor, and Tucker," Mom said. "I start in three weeks!"

Still, nobody said anything. Max opened the doughnut box and took one with sprinkles and strawberry frosting.

"Come on, kids," Dad prompted us. "Isn't this exciting for Mommy? Don't you have anything to say to her?"

"Thank you for doughnuts!" Max piped up. He obviously had no idea how much everything was about to change.

But I did.

"Why?" I asked.

It wasn't what Dad was hoping for—I could tell by the way he frowned at me, his forehead all wrinkly—but sometimes the first thing that pops into my brain is also the first thing that pops out of my mouth.

"Well . . ." Mom was flustered, and that was strange. "I mean, I was always going to go back to work someday. And Max is going into pre-K this year, so the timing makes sense."

Dad was still looking at me, and then he said, "Also, I lost my job."

"Rob!" Mom exclaimed. "We weren't going to tell them yet, we agreed—"

"Look at her," Dad interrupted, gesturing at me. "She's about five minutes away from figuring it out."

Max took another doughnut.

"You got *fired*?" I asked.

"Not exactly. I didn't do anything wrong," Dad replied. "The company's in bad shape, and it's probably going to close. Uncle Craig's company has been struggling, too. That's why he decided to take that job in California."

"Hang on," I said. "How long have you known about this?"

Mom and Dad exchanged another glance. "Six months, I suppose," Dad said.

"And you're just telling us *now*?" I exclaimed. My face was getting really hot, like my skin was as mad as the rest of me. "Is this why I had to stop taking art classes? Will *we* have to move?"

Mom got up and moved next to me. My shoulders went stiff when she wrapped her arm around them, but she gave me a squeeze, anyway. "It's true we've been watching our budget a little more carefully. And we didn't want you to worry while we figured out what was going to happen next," she said. "I remember when my dad lost his job. It was really scary."

"I'd rather be scared than lied to," I said.

Mom took her arm back. "Well, we made the best decision we could with the information we had," she said. "And now that we know what's happening next, we're telling you two. And no, we don't have any plans to move."

"Just because it's a change doesn't mean it's going to be a bad thing," Dad said.

I thought about that for a moment. "So . . . you'll be home with us after school?" I asked him.

"Actually, you'll both be in an after-school program," Mom said. "Max will be in Little Learners, and I signed you up for Run Wild! last night."

"The running club?" I howled. "Do you even know me?"

"It'll be interesting to try something new!" Mom said.

"But I *hate* running!" I said. "You know that!"

"Since when?" she asked, baffled.

"Since forever!" I said. "When was the last time you saw me run anywhere? Running? *Seriously?*"

"I'm sorry," Mom said. "Everything else was already full."

So the truth comes out, I thought, but at least this time, I was smart enough to *think* it instead of *say* it.

"And it's only until December," Mom continued, like she was measuring out each word. "Then we can sign you up for a new after-school elective for January."

"So this is . . . permanent?" I asked. That's when it hit me. Mom wasn't going back to work as, like, a substitute teacher. She meant it. Like, really meant it. I turned to Dad. "How come we can't stay home with you in the afternoons?"

"Well, hopefully, I'll find another full-time job soon," Dad replied. "But until then, I'll need to be available for job interviews. And I'm hoping to pick up a little work in the gig economy."

"The *what* economy?" I said.

"The gig economy, baby!" Dad said in a too-cheerful voice. "You know, driving people around, delivering packages. That sort of thing."

"Couldn't I come with you?" I asked hopefully.

Mom and Dad looked at each other instead of saying no. So I grabbed my chance. "Please, please, please," I begged. "I hate running, so much. I'm so bad at it, and it makes my legs hurt and my lungs hurt and my—"

"Okay, okay, okay," Dad said, laughing as he held up his hands. "You can come with me."

Just when I was about to start cheering, Mom jumped in.

"Only until Run Wild! starts in the second week of school," Mom added quickly. "That's the plan."

"It's still work, Abby," Dad replied. "I need to take it seriously, like any other job."

"I know, I know," I said. "I won't get in the way. Promise." But secretly, I knew I just needed a chance. I'd be the best helper; Dad would get way more done when I came along! I was imagining how we'd drive around Winston-Salem, music blaring, when I flopped back in my seat and accidentally bumped my head on the wall. "Ow!"

I hated the way everyone stared at me, looking all sympathetic and sorry, so I pointed at Max's plate, which was piled high with doughnuts. "How many doughnuts are you going to let him eat, exactly?"

I didn't really care. My appetite was zero.

Ratzit!

❋ ❋ ❋

Heyyyy Z,

I guess you're on an airplane right now. TAKE ME WITH YOU! I should have snuck into your suitcase when I had the chance. Mom and Dad just dropped a big stupid bomb on our whole family. Mom is going back to work as a paralegal, which is like a lawyer's helper, and Dad has some gig job thing (???), and they signed me up for the Run Wild! club totally against my will—Can you even?! Max is too little to get it. He's excited about doing Little Learners because of the snacks. Please! Anyway, I have one week to prove that I can help Dad with his gig thing and get out of Run Wild! forever. Keep your fingers crossed.

Something else also happened. Did you ever get a bump? Or two? Like on your chest? Is that supposed to happen right before fourth grade starts? Just wondering!!!

Write back soon. I miss youuuuuuu!

Then I drew, like, a million hearts and signed it with a big blue *A*. I'd already memorized Zoe's new address, so I wrote it on the envelope, stuck a stamp in the corner, and sealed it with my best glitter stickers.

I did the math in my head. If it took, hmm, four days for my letter to get to California, and Zoe wrote back the day she got it, because of course she would, and then it took four days for *her* letter to come back to me . . .

Well, eight days wasn't too long to wait, was it?

CHAPTER 3

I t turned out that eight days was too long to wait. Two days was too long, even. By day three, I was going through serious Zoe withdrawal. Mom could tell by the way I moped and flopped around the house. I was lying on my bed with my head hanging over the edge and my hair brushing against the floor when she came into my room.

"Uh-oh," Mom said. "This is worse than I thought."

"What is?" I asked, staring at the wall.

"You have a serious case of summeritis," she said. "You look bored to tears."

Yeah, I was bored, but that wasn't why I felt like crying.

"There's only three more weeks until school starts," Mom continued. "Let's make the most of summer while we still can! Why don't you set up a mud-pie station for Max in the backyard? Or make a vision board from my old maga-zines? Or plan something yummy to bake for dessert?"

I shrugged, but since I was hanging off the bed, my shoulders went down instead of up.

"I know!" Mom said. "Why don't you invite a friend over to hang out?"

"I have no friends," I said.

"Oh, Abby. You know that's not true," she said. I could tell she was getting frustrated with me. And she was right. I did have friends, lots of friends. But . . . none of them were Zoe. And none of them were a *best* friend. Besides, it felt pretty random to call someone I hadn't even seen since school got out in June.

Mom sat down on the bed, making the mattress dip. She held her phone in front of my upside-down face. "Well, if you don't want to call a friend . . . would you like to call Zoe?"

I scrambled up and felt all the extra blood whoosh out of my head. "Really?" I exclaimed.

"Of course," Mom said, glancing at the clock. "It's mid-morning in California. I'm sure everyone's up."

Mom tapped the screen of her phone, and the next

thing I knew, she was talking to Aunt Rachel. "Listen, is Zoe around? Abby's dying to talk to her."

Then Mom held out her phone. I grabbed it and stuck it to my ear.

"Hello? Abby?"

"Zoe!" I shrieked. Just hearing her voice made me feel a thousand times happier. Mom was smiling, too, as she slipped out of my room. "I miss you! How is everything? What's it like in California?"

"Sunny. Busy. Different," she said. "The moving truck isn't here yet, so we don't have any of our stuff. Just what we put in our suitcases."

"Really?" I asked.

"Really. We don't even have dishes. We're using so many paper plates, we'll have to plant, like, a hundred trees to make up for it. And the house—"

"Is it amazing?" I asked, cutting her off by accident.

"It's all *white* inside," she said. "White walls and white ceilings and white floors. There's, like, no color anywhere."

"Ugh," I said, remembering how Zoe's old house was a mix of a million colors that all seemed to swirl together just right.

"But we already went to the hardware store and got paint chips," she continued. "You should do that sometime—you'd love it! There are so many colors! And you can tape them up on your wall to decide which color looks best. They can even make a custom color for you and match anything you want, like a scarf or nail polish or a flower or anything."

"Wow," I said. "That's so cool. What color are you going to paint your new room?"

"Purple," she said right away. "Or pink. Either purple with blue or pink with green. Or maybe purple with pink?"

I smiled, not that Zoe could see.

She talked on and on, describing her new room and house and yard and pool until I felt like I was right there with her. At last, she said, "So what's new in Winston-Salem?"

Now that was a good question. What *was* new in Winston-Salem?

"Nothing," I started to say. Except there was one *big* thing that I was dying to ask Zoe about. I'd written about it in my letter. *Would it be weird to talk about it on the phone?* I wondered. No, of course not. This was *Zoe*. We could talk about *anything*. And we usually did.

So why did the words feel stuck in my throat?

"Actually, there is one thing, Z," I started. Before I said anything else, I walked across the room to close my door all the way—just as Max stomped in.

"Is that *Zoe*?" he yelled excitedly. "Can I talk? Can I talk? Hey, Zoe, can you hear meeeeee?"

"Get out," I mouthed.

"You still there?" Zoe asked.

"Yeah . . . just . . . hold on . . ."

I held the phone away from my mouth. "*Out*," I whispered in the maddest voice I had.

"Why can't I talk?" Max whined.

Then I heard Zoe again. "Abby? Hang on," she said.

I pointed at my door, but Max ignored me. Like usual.

There was a long pause before Zoe spoke again.

"Listen, Abby, I've gotta go," she said. "My mom wants her phone back, and we're going shopping for stuff for my room. Next time, call me on *my* phone!"

"Right. Duh," I said. "I think my mom forgot you had one."

"I'm so glad you called," Zoe said. "I really miss you."

"I miss you, too," I said, and suddenly, a million different words welled up in my chest. I could've talked and talked and talked to Zoe for hours. For days.

"Love you!" Zoe said.

"Love you, too," I said. "Wait, just one more thing—"

But Zoe had already disconnected.

"I wanted to talk to Zoe," Max said, pouting.

I thought about yelling for Mom, but what was the point? She couldn't do anything now.

"Zoe had to go," I told Max, giving him a little push toward the door. "And so do you."

The minute Max left, I made sure my door was shut supertight. I glanced at Mom's phone, wishing Zoe and I could've talked just a little longer. Wishing I could've asked her the big question I couldn't stop thinking about.

At least she'll get my letter any day now, I thought. *Maybe even today! And then she'll write back, and I'll write back to her, and she'll write back again . . .*

It wasn't going to be the same. But it would still be okay.

❀ ❀ ❀

Eight days had already passed. Then two more. Then four more days passed—it had been two whole weeks! And no letter from Zoe. There was only one explanation. My letter must have gotten lost in the mail. Ratzit! Thanks for nothing, flamingos!

So I wrote to Zoe again, telling her all about ordering back-to-school clothes online this year, and how much I loved my new blue sweater with the little ruffle at the bottom, and asking her what she going to wear for the first day of school. Do they even wear sweaters in California, or is it all tank tops and sundresses? I tried to ask a lot of questions in my second letter. I wanted to make it easy for her to write back.

I didn't get a letter from Zoe, but I did get a postcard from Miller Elementary School. It was a big deal to find out who my teacher would be for fourth grade. Last year, Zoe had Mrs. Jacobson, who was the nicest, smartest, greatest teacher in the whole school. She never yelled, and she never, ever gave homework over the breaks. I had spent the entire summer daydreaming about being in Mrs. Jacobson's class. I had wished on every star (even the ones that weren't shooting across the sky) and every clover (even the ones that only had three leaves).

So why did my postcard say MR. SMILEY?

Who *was* Mr. Smiley, anyway?

I couldn't remember any teachers named Mr. Smiley. So he must be new. If Zoe still lived around the corner, I would have run all the way to her house, and we would have compared postcards and talked all about Mr. Smiley and whoever her fifth-grade teacher was. I mean, would've been. Because Zoe didn't go to Miller Elementary anymore. I didn't even know what her new school was called.

That postcard with MR. SMILEY typed on it was the signal that summer was over. This year, the first day of school was a bigger deal than ever before. Because it was also the first day of work for Mom. And when the morning arrived, she seemed more nervous than me!

The whole house felt like a tornado of chaos was ripping through it as everyone tried to get ready. Mom was rushing from room to room, yelling at everybody and nobody. "Who's not dressed yet? Who needs help? Rob, this is why we needed to pack the lunches *last* night and not wait until the morning!"

"Don't worry," Dad called out. "We're right on time."

Dad always said that, even when we were running way late. I leaned closer to the mirror so I could figure out if my hair looked better tucked behind my ears or loose in front of them. It's lucky for Mom that I can get ready all by myself and don't need help from anybody.

Unfortunately, the same is not true for Max.

He wandered into my room, wearing only his underpants, one sock, and his favorite monster shirt. I stared at him for a second. "Max," I finally said. "Aren't you forgetting something?"

Max shrugged.

"Pants," I said. Then louder. "You need *pants*, Max. You can't go to school without pants."

"I'm very busy right now," he said. "I have to take care of my pet."

"What pet?" I asked, scrunching up my face. We had no pets, even though I asked for a kitten pretty much every day.

Max held up a Ziploc bag that was all puffed out with air. "My pet," he repeated.

"Your pet . . . is a plastic bag?" I asked.

"Yup," he said.

I decided to play along. "Okay, what's . . . its . . . name?"

Max stared at the bag. "Pet," he finally said.

"Your pet is a plastic bag named Pet?"

"Yes," Max said. "Meet Pet."

"Kids! You need to be ready to go in five minutes!" Mom called from the kitchen.

"Great to meet you, Pet," I said. "But, Max, you've got to put on some pants. I'm serious."

"I can't," he said. "Pet needs me."

I stared at the empty plastic bag. "Pet looks good to me," I said. "You, however, are pants-less, and that is a problem."

Max shook Pet at my face. "But Pet's hungry!" he said. "He hasn't had any breakfast!"

This was getting ridiculous. "What does Pet eat?" I asked.

"Money."

I made my eyes go squinty. "Seriously?"

Max nodded.

I sighed, took two quarters from the last time the tooth fairy came, and shoved them at Max. "Here," I said.

Max stuffed the quarters into Pet. Now Pet went *clink, clink, clink* whenever Max moved him. I helped Max finish getting dressed, super speedy, and then we ran to the front door.

"Ready!" we yelled at the same time.

Mom was hopping down the hallway as she put on her shoes. I thought she'd be so happy to see us all ready to go, but she didn't even notice that I'd helped Max get dressed.

"Abby," she began. "What are you wearing? It's going to be ninety degrees today."

I looked down at my brand-new blue sweater. "This is my favorite new outfit. It's perfect for the first day of school."

"Yes, but . . . ," Mom said, "you're going to be so hot. I really think you should change clothes."

"But, Mom," I said. "I've been planning this outfit for weeks! I don't want to wear something else!"

Mom opened her mouth and closed it and glanced at the clock. "Okay, fine." She sighed. "I don't have time to argue. Come on, let's go."

The minute we stepped outside, it felt like I'd walked into a wall of sunshine. It was way hotter than I expected. *Maybe I should change.* The thought flickered through my head so fast, I couldn't stop it. I glanced back at the house, but Mom was already buckling her seat belt. The engine went *vroom-vroom-vroom* as she started the car. And then she honked the horn.

It won't feel so hot at school, I thought as I scrambled into the back seat.

But boy, was I wrong.

✿ ✿ ✿

When I got to Mr. Smiley's classroom, each desk had a name on it. I did a speed walk down each row because I couldn't wait to find out which friends were in my class. Hopefully, they weren't all in Mrs. Jacobson's class. That would definitely be a double-ratzit surprise!

Some names I was happy to see, like Maya and Reese and Ebony, who were all nice and would always make room, no matter where they were sitting in the cafeteria. Some names I was not so happy to see, like Anderson, who stuck a wad of chewed-up gum in my hair in second grade. I was *still* mad about it.

And then there was Savannah. She had been the queen of third grade, and I was sure she'd be the queen of fourth grade, too. I didn't know if I was happy to see her in my class or not. It would all depend on whether Savannah was happy to see *me*.

"Find your name and take your seat."

I jumped. I hadn't noticed Mr. Smiley come into the room. I wasn't the only one out of my seat, but I scrambled over there like I'd gotten in trouble.

For someone named Smiley, my new teacher seemed like a big grump. He didn't smile as other kids arrived. He barely even looked at us.

We sat in perfect silence, waiting for the school day to start. That's when I noticed the walls. They were covered with maps—many more than the usual map of the United States. There was a map of Winston-Salem and another one of North Carolina, and a map of all the countries in Africa, and a weird-looking one with lots of different colorful lines on it that said NEW YORK CITY SUBWAY. There was even a map of the whole world as if it had been sliced up and stretched flat.

The bell rang, and everyone was sitting, and Mr. Smiley *still* hadn't smiled. "Welcome to fourth grade. If elementary school were a marathon, you're entering the final lap," he announced.

What did that even mean?

Mr. Smiley pushed a button and the SMART Board flickered to life. There was a big, bold word on it: *CHANGE*.

"Things change in fourth grade," Mr. Smiley continued. "Letter grades, for example. Science fair. Geography bee.

In fourth grade everything counts. Neatness. Penmanship. Effort. In fourth grade you're going to work harder. Think deeper. And, I hope, learn more than ever before."

I gulped. Zoe wasn't kidding last year when she said fourth grade was *tough*.

The cursor started blinking in the middle of the word, and then Mr. Smiley added some letters. Now it said *CHALLENGE*.

"I know you can all rise to the challenge," Mr. Smiley said.

Can we? I wondered.

"Okay!" Mr. Smiley said. "Close your notebooks and zip up your backpacks. It's time for a quiz!"

There it was. Mr. Smiley's first smile. Does it make somebody evil if the only thing that gets them smiling is a surprise quiz? A *surprise* quiz on the *first* day of school? That was absolutely, positively evil! Mrs. Jacobson would *never* give a quiz on the first day of school. I just knew it.

But Mr. Smiley was already passing out the quizzes like it was no big deal. He was even whistling a little bit. Whistling! Like he was having a great time!

"Ratzit," I whispered to myself. Maya looked like she was going to cry.

"Now, this quiz should not be stressing you out," Mr. Smiley announced. Easy for him to say! "This is to help me understand where we need to start with math."

"How about the beginning?" Garrett cracked. But no one laughed.

Mr. Smiley raised his bushy eyebrows at Garrett, but all he said was, "You have fifteen minutes."

I glanced down at the neat rows of problems, addition and subtraction and even some multiplication and division. That's when it started: prickly, tickly tingles under my arms. Then on my back, and my chest, and the palms of my hands. It was like a wave of heat washed over me, and suddenly, I was sitting there, sweating in my sweater.

$11 \times 12 = $ _____

I kind of tugged and pulled at the sweater, hoping it would mop up the sweat. But I could feel wet beads sliding down my back, like big fat raindrops rolling down a windowpane.

$1/4 + 3/8 = $ _____

Ignore the sweat, I told myself. But that turned out to be impossible. Not only could I feel it, all of a sudden, I realized that I could *smell* it. At first, I thought it was something else. I mean, Matt was obviously wearing the same stinky sneakers from last year. Or maybe someone brought a smelly lunch, something with spicy salami or a hard-boiled egg. Or a cheese sandwich, sweating as much as I was in the humid classroom.

I moved my hand up like I was scratching my shoulder and stuck my finger under my armpit. It was wet! Wet with sweat!!! *Whyyyyyyy?* I thought in total agony. This had never happened to me before. Why now, on the first day of school, was I sweating like a sweaty swamp monster?

Across the aisle Maya sniffed loudly. Was it allergies—or had she just caught a whiff of *me*? If I could smell myself, could everybody else? Did they know it was *me*?

Ratzit, ratzit, ratzit, I thought.

My brain was practically doing somersaults trying to figure out what to do next. Mom always says there are plenty of options in any situation, no matter what. The big challenge is to figure out what they are. And of course, some are better than others. Like, even though I wanted to run out of the room so fast that I made an Abby-shaped hole in the door, I should probably not do that. For one thing, it would only make me sweat more.

"Time's up!" Mr. Smiley announced. For a horrible moment I thought he meant I was out of time to figure out a plan. But he was really talking about the quiz.

Everyone started passing their papers forward. I clenched my elbows against my sides, hoping to lock in the sweat and the smell.

But I couldn't sit like a frozen statue all day long. Eventually I would have to, like, move.

That's when I had an idea. I raised my hand—not high, because I was pretty sure that everyone would see the damp spots under my armpits if I did, but high enough to get Mr. Smiley's attention.

"Yes . . . Abby?" he asked.

"Bathroom?" I squeaked.

He nodded once and handed me a bathroom pass. I scrambled out of my seat and flew to the door.

The quiet hallway was about a million degrees cooler than my classroom. Luckily, the bathroom was only three doors down from my class. I wanted to press my hot face

45

against the cold tile walls, but I didn't, because gross. It may have been amazingly cool and perfectly peaceful, but it was still a bathroom, you know?

Instead, I went over to the sink and splashed some cold water on my face. It felt so good, I didn't even care that I kind of messed up my hair. I was worried that my hand still smelled like armpit sweat, so I washed it really good with soap.

Then I had my genius idea. The one Mom always promised would come whenever I was in a tricky situation. If I could wash my *hands*, why not my *armpits*, too?

I glanced over at the door. I'd have to be fast. I didn't want anyone to see me having a mini bath in the sink. I squashed up some paper towels with water and soap and shoved them up under my sweater. The soap in the school bathroom had a strong lemon smell, but I figured smelling like lemons could only be an improvement.

I stared at myself in the mirror. Maybe it was the cool water, or the peace of being all alone in the bathroom, but I didn't feel panicky and queasy anymore.

There were water droplets splattered all over my sweater, but they'd dry soon enough. My hair was damp and stringy, but it would dry, too. It was the first day of fourth grade. My new teacher seemed like a big meanie, I'd probably failed the first quiz of the year, and my favorite sweater smelled like a cross between a locker room and a soap factory.

I wasn't going to jinx things by declaring they couldn't get any worse.

But if they did, I'd find a way to handle it.

I had to.

CHAPTER 4

After school, I *almost* forgot how much I hate running till I spotted Dad's car in the car line. The minute my name was called, I raced over and leaped into the back seat. It was so jammed with packages that there was barely room for me, but the air-conditioning was on full blast so I couldn't complain.

"Hey, biscuit!" Dad said. "How was the first day of school?"

I raised my eyebrows. We'd already been through this when he tried to call me "cookie."

"Whoops, sorry. I forgot." Dad laughed. "No food names."

I tried not to show how surprised I was by Dad's clothes. He was wearing a uniform—gray pants with a matching gray shirt with blue stripes on the sleeves, and a name tag, too. It was way different from the button-down shirts and ties he used to wear to work.

Dad grinned as he pretended to brush imaginary dust off his shoulder. "Not bad, huh? I feel pretty official in my new threads."

"You better be careful, or Max will take your name tag," I joked.

"No kidding," Dad replied. He tossed a granola bar at me and said, "Buckle up! We're holding up the line, and I've got a lot of deliveries to make. Welcome to Dad's Delivery Service!"

"You have to deliver *all* these? Today?" I asked, gesturing at the packages.

"Not just today—within the next couple hours," he replied. "Technically, I have until eight p.m., but I'd rather be done before we need to pick up Max."

I shook my head. Unless he had some kind of magic teleportation power, I didn't see how that would be possible.

"Oh, ye of little faith," Dad said with a laugh. "Come on! I've got the GPS all fired up, and with my best backseat driver helping me navigate, we can get it done."

Dad cranked up some tunes, and we both sang along as loud as we wanted without anybody telling us to dial it back, like, just a bit. The drive was all stops and starts, one brown cardboard box after another. Big ones, little ones, light ones, heavy ones. Little by little, one box at a time, the car started to empty.

We only had about ten boxes left when a familiar address popped up: 1240 Creek Street. "Hey, I think I know this house," I told Dad. "This is where Mrs. Flamingo lives."

"Mrs. Flamingo?" Dad asked.

"That's not her real name," I explained. "That's just what Zoe and I call her. She has a huge flock of flamingos in her yard. Not real ones, the plastic kind. And she puts them in funny poses and dresses them up for the holidays."

"What a time to be alive," Dad replied.

I found the package for Mrs. Flamingo and learned that her real name is actually Daphne Jackson. *I can't wait to tell Zoe*, I thought.

Then things got even more exciting. As Dad pulled up in front of Mrs. Flamingo's—I mean, Mrs. Jackson's—house, I saw her outside!

And she was getting the flamingos ready for back to school!

"Wow," I said under my breath. This was so cool. If only Zoe—

I shook my head. Zoe couldn't be here, so I'd just have to make sure I memorized every detail and write her a long, long, loooong letter later.

"Dad," I said. "Can I carry this one up?"

He glanced at me in the rearview mirror. "Well . . . ," he began.

"Please," I added quickly. "I've been watching you. I know I can do it!"

"Okay—let's give it a try." He grinned. "So, here's what you do. Bring the package up to the front door, then use my phone to take a picture to prove that we delivered it. Got it?"

"Got it," I said.

I tucked the box under one arm and held Dad's phone in my hand. Then I walked up the path, admiring all the flamingos wearing little backpacks. There was a big addition to the yard, too—a flamingo-size school bus!

"Can I help you?"

It was Mrs. Flamingo herself! She was standing behind the bus, trying to wrangle a flamingo into the driver's seat.

"Oh! Hi! I love your flamingos!" Whoops—I was babbling. "I mean, I have a package for you. It's right here."

I held out the package, but Mrs. Flamingo didn't move to take it.

"What's the name on it?" she finally asked.

"Uh . . . ," I began. "It says 'Daphne Jackson.'"

Mrs. Flamingo shook her head. "That's not me," she said. "That's my niece. She doesn't live here."

I glanced back at the car, but Dad just grinned and gave me a thumbs-up.

"Um . . . where does she live?" I asked. I guessed we'd have to make a special delivery, but I didn't know how that would work with the delivery app. Maybe I needed to get Dad.

All of a sudden, Mrs. Flamingo looked sad and frustrated and something else altogether that I couldn't figure out. She pointed at a rusty old car parked in the driveway.

"The car?" I asked.

Mrs. Flamingo nodded. Then she went back to her flamingos.

This was definitely way out of my league. And a complication like this was *not* good for my plan to get out of running club. I hurried back to the car and opened the door.

"How'd it go, kiddo?" Dad asked.

"Delivery failure," I replied as I handed him the package and told him what Mrs. Flamingo had said.

Dad nodded slowly. "Let me see if I can get a little more information," he said. "Sit tight."

I slumped down in the car and watched out the window as Dad, package under *his* arm this time, walked up to Mrs. Flamingo. They had a long chat. Too long for a simple delivery, I thought. I lowered the window, hoping I could listen in, but I couldn't hear anything clearly.

At last Dad put the package by the front door and took a picture. I noticed right away that he was especially quiet when he came back to the car.

"So . . . what was that about?" I asked.

There was a long pause. "It's kind of complicated," Dad finally said. "Basically, Daphne Jackson is living out of her car right now, so she uses her aunt's address for deliveries."

"She *lives* in her *car*?" I couldn't hide my surprise, even if I wanted to. "But why? Why can't she just live with her aunt?"

"That, I don't know," Dad told me. "But family relationships can be, well, complicated."

"But why her *car*?" I said. "Why not an apartment or something?"

Dad sighed like he was frustrated, but when he spoke, I could tell he wasn't upset with me. "We have something called 'a housing crisis' in the city right now," he explained. "That means there's a lot of fancy, expensive housing and not enough affordable housing for people who aren't really rich."

"But we're not really rich," I said.

"No," Dad agreed. "Mom and I bought our house a long time ago, when it was more affordable. Things are different now."

I didn't say anything. There were too many thoughts ping-ponging around my brain.

"So, if Daphne Jackson is living in her car, does that mean she's homeless?" I finally asked.

"Yes," Dad said quietly. "I think it does."

Now we were both quiet. Everything felt wrong. We were zooming all over town in a car crammed with packages, while Daphne's car was basically her *home*.

"That's not right," I said, surprising myself with how mad and loud my voice was.

"No," Dad replied. "It's not."

"What are people doing to fix it?"

Dad sighed again. "It's not an easy problem to fix," he began.

"Of course it is!" I argued. "If people need houses, then we should build them."

Dad looked at me in the mirror and smiled, one of those crinkly sad smiles that always makes me want to give him a big hug. "It should be that easy," he replied. "But it's not. Land is expensive, especially here. Building is expensive. And people who are homeless . . ."

"Can't afford it," I finished for him.

"Yes," Dad said.

I didn't have anything left to say, and I guess Dad didn't, either. As we left Mrs. Flamingo's to make the next delivery, I stared out the window at the buildings zipping past.

That night I was so tired, I thought I'd fall right asleep, but I was wronger than wrong. When I closed my eyes, I imagined Mrs. Flamingo's flamingos, all lined up near that car where Daphne *lived*. I imagined I could still see Mr. Smiley's giant eyebrows all scrunched together, glaring at me. I imagined

I could still feel the sweat prickling across my skin. I imagined I could still smell the stinky perfume of lemony soap, woolly sweater, and sweat.

No, that one was real. I'd changed my clothes the instant I got home, and flung my sweater into the corner because I didn't know what else to do with it. Even though I was all snuggled up in my bed across the room, I could definitely still smell it. Yuck.

No wonder I couldn't sleep. And—I'd never admit this, not even to Zoe—but I kind of didn't want to be alone. Not with all those cringey memories of my day flickering through my brain like a movie I didn't want to watch. I had so many worries. They were like a brick wall that I just couldn't get over.

I got up and poked my head into the hall. The kitchen light was still on, which meant either Mom or Dad was still awake. I kind of hoped it would be Mom.

It's funny how much quieter you can be at night, without even really trying. I crept down the hallway to the kitchen, practically tiptoeing, even though I didn't mean to. It *was* Mom, staring at her laptop and sipping a cup of tea. The light from the laptop in the dim kitchen made her face look kind of blue.

"Hey," I said, leaning against the doorway like it was no big deal for me to be awake at ten o'clock at night.

She jumped anyway. "Abby! Why are you out of bed?"

I shrugged. It was really weird how Mom was the only person in the world I wanted to talk to, but now that we were right here together, finally alone, I didn't know where to begin. "What are you doing?" I asked. "Working?"

"Something like that," Mom said with one of those smiles that wasn't really a smile. "One of the other paralegals told me that Mr. Tucker likes to send us to-do lists right before he goes to bed. She was right."

I craned my neck to get a look, but Mom closed her laptop and pulled a chair out from the table. "You want to sit?"

I shrugged again and stared down at my feet.

"Toast," Mom said suddenly. "I could really go for some toast right now. You want some?"

I shrugged one more time, but this time it was more of a sure-why-not? shrug. Mom was pretty smart. She could tell the difference.

"Butter or jam?"

Tough question.

"Or both?" Mom continued.

"Both," I said. "Definitely."

Mom will tell you herself that she is not the best cook, so it's not like I'm insulting her or anything when I say that. But she is excellent at making toast. Outstanding, even. Soon, the whole kitchen was filled with the golden smell of toasted bread and creamy melted butter and the sweetness of raspberry jam. I took a bite of the toast, all hot and buttery and berrylicious, and that wall of worries came tumbling down, just in time for my words to come tumbling out. I told Mom *everything*, from Mr. Smiley's caterpillar eyebrows to the surprise sweat attack during the quiz. At one point she kind of said *hmmmphhh* and brushed her hand across her mouth, like she was maybe trying to cover a laugh, but I think she was just wiping crumbs off her chin.

"I feel like my body *betrayed* me," I finally said.

"Betrayed you? By sweating?" Mom asked.

I nodded.

"No, no, no," Mom said. Her voice was kind but also firm, so I knew she meant business. "Bodies are supposed to sweat! That's what they do. It's really neat, actually. When you get too hot, your brain will activate all your sweat glands to release moisture, which evaporates to cool off your core internal temperature—"

I forced myself not to groan. "Okay, okay, really neat," I interrupted her. "But why does it have to *smell*?"

Mom looked thoughtful for a moment. "That's not actually the sweat," she said. "There's billions of tiny bacteria on your skin, and *that's* what makes your sweat smell."

I flopped forward so that my forehead banged onto the table. This was just getting worse and worse.

"Hey," Mom said, rubbing my shoulder. "There's no reason to be so upset. Everybody sweats, sweetie. Everybody! I can get you some deodorant if it bothers you. You can use it if you want—or not. It's up to you."

It wasn't just the sweating, though. It was everything—Zoe being gone and the way Mr. Smiley never smiled and now my new favorite sweater smelled like sweat and bathroom soap, probably forever. Bathroom soap!

And the one that was almost too big and sad to think about: Mrs. Flamingo's niece, living in her car.

I was going to sigh, but it came out sounding more like a pitiful little whimper.

"Oh, Abby," Mom murmured as she wrapped her arm around me. A bright flash of gratitude lit up my whole heart. Mom loved me, no matter how stinky or smelly or bacteria-y I was.

"It's not just sweat." It kind of sounded like I was choking on my words. "It's also—"

Mom waited. It didn't get any easier to tell her about the bumps the more time passed. I probably should have told her three weeks ago.

Then I thought about how relieved Aunt Rachel was to find out that her lump was no big deal. So, crossing my fingers for hope, I took a deep breath.

"Mom," I whispered. "I have these bumps."

A pause.

"Where?" she asked. Carefully. Delicately.

I waved my hand in front of my chest.

"Oh," Mom said. Just *Oh*. "Do they, um, hurt?"

I nodded. "Sometimes. Not all the time. And not bad. Just . . ."

"You know they're there?" Mom guessed.

I nodded again.

"Well," she said. "Well, I, uh, I don't think it's anything to worry about. My guess is it's just the next part of growing up—like a growth spurt or losing your baby teeth. But here's what we'll do. In the morning I'll call Dr. Camfield, and we'll go in for a little visit."

My stomach squashed that toast so hard, it practically went back up my throat. "Do you think they're lumps? Like the one Aunt Rachel had?" There. I'd *finally* found the courage to ask.

"No! Oh, Abby, no," Mom said, folding me into another hug. "That would be very, very, very unlikely at your age. Has that been worrying you?"

"Yeah," I said into her shoulder. "Kind of."

"Well, put those worries out of your head right now," she ordered me. "And that's why we're going to see Dr. Camfield. She's an expert, you know. She'll be able to put my mind at ease."

"Your mind?" I asked.

Mom laughed, covering her mouth as her laugh turned into a yawn. "I meant *your* mind, sweet pea," she told me. "Sorry. I think the first day was exhausting for both of us."

Mom's yawn must have been the contagious kind, because I was suddenly yawning, too—the kind of yawn that was so gigantic, it felt like it would crack my head in half.

"We should both go to bed," Mom said, glancing at the clock on the microwave.

"Okay," I said.

This time, I really did fall right asleep.

✽　✽　✽

Dr. Camfield has been my doctor since I was a little baby. Two days later I was sitting on the exam table waiting for her, wearing one of those loose gowns that looks like a pillowcase with sleeves, swinging my feet back and forth. I liked the hollow, metallic noise my heels made when they hit the edge of the table. I liked it so much, I barely realized I was doing it.

"Abby," Mom said, pressing her temples. "Please, don't."

"Don't what?" I asked, confused.

Mom gestured at my swinging legs. I pushed my hands down on my knees to make them stop. Without the twangy metallic thunk, the room seemed creepy-quiet, but I guess that's what Mom liked. A creepy-quiet room.

Down the hall, in the distance, a baby started crying. Mom winced and made a face of sympathy. "Shots, I bet," she said. "Oh, you used to cry so hard when you got your shots. Your whole body would shake, and your face would turn bright red."

It almost seemed like Mom was talking more to herself than to me, so I stayed very quiet so I wouldn't break the spell. I loved it when she told stories from when I was little—all the things that I just couldn't remember, no matter how hard I tried.

"And I'd cry, too," she said. "I couldn't help myself, even though the nurses would sort of laugh at—"

There was a brisk knock at the door, which swung open right as Mom said, "Come in."

"Abby!" Dr. Camfield exclaimed with a big smile. She always looked—and acted—like I was her favorite patient ever, even though she usually saw me at my worst—when my head was clogged up with snot or my throat was covered in blisters.

Or now, when I was suddenly getting all bumpy and stinky.

"Look at you, big fourth grader," she continued. "You're getting tall! How's school?"

"Good," I said. "It's, you know, school."

Dr. Camfield laughed like I had just told a really funny joke. "Isn't that the truth," she said. "So, what brings you in today? Not sick, I hope?"

I looked at Mom and tried to radio her with my mind. *You tell her. You tell her. You tell her.*

She must have gotten the message, because she cleared her throat and said, "Well, we just wanted to check in with you because Abby's started to notice some, ah, some changes."

"Okay," Dr. Camfield said. "What kind of changes?"

This time, Mom nodded at me, and I knew that even if she received my mind-radioed message, she wouldn't listen to it. So I told Dr. Camfield about my sweaty armpits and— *gulp*—my bumps.

"Abby, is it okay with you if I feel your chest?" Dr. Camfield asked.

"Sure," I said.

Dr. Camfield's fingers felt like a butterfly brushing the gown over my skin. She was super gentle as she touched all around my nipples.

"Tender?" she asked, looking down.

"Sometimes," I said. "If I lie down on my stomach."

Dr. Camfield wasn't surprised. "Abby, these bumps that you feel? They're breast buds," she explained. "That's the first stage of breast development."

"So . . . they're not bad?" I asked.

Dr. Camfield smiled reassuringly. "Not bad at all," she said. "This is one of the signs that you've started puberty."

Puberty.

Puberty.

That big, serious, weird, *embarrassing* word just sat there, hanging in the air.

Dr. Camfield didn't look worried, but Mom sure did. "Are you sure?" she asked in a low voice. "She's so young—she's not even going to turn ten for another few months."

"Abby's right on schedule," Dr. Camfield said, and I kind of got the feeling that maybe her reassuring voice was for Mom more than it was for me. "It starts earlier for girls today than it did for us."

"I just thought . . . we had more time . . . ," Mom said.

More time for what? I wondered. I'd have to remember to ask Mom later.

"You're not alone," Dr. Camfield said. "It's a process, though, and different for everyone. And it doesn't happen overnight, even though it seems that way if we're not paying attention."

Dr. Camfield opened a drawer, rummaged around, and pulled out a notepad. "You may have noticed some other changes happening to your body, Abby," she told me. "It's normal to have mixed feelings. Some girls are excited. Others are nervous, or feel like they aren't ready yet. And some feel all of the above!"

Check, check, and check, I thought.

For a minute the only sound was Dr. Camfield's pen scribbling on the pad.

"Here are some books about puberty I really like," she said as she tore off the page. "They might help answer your questions, or help you prepare for what's coming next. But the most important thing, in my experience"—and here Dr. Camfield was talking to Mom again—"is keeping the lines of communication open."

"Abby and I talk all the time," Mom said.

Do we? I wondered. I mean, yes, about what's for dinner and if I finished my homework and if I remembered to clean my room. But when it came to real talking, about important stuff . . . Well, that was a lot harder. For a lot of reasons.

"Excellent," Dr. Camfield said, smiling. "Just keep it up."

✿　✿　✿

"You know, the car is a good place to have conversations," Mom said as she drove down the street.

"Mm," I said, staring out the window. She didn't have to say that. I could tell the whole way home that Mom wanted to talk to me. I mean, she wanted to *talk* to me. But all my words—and even my feelings—were so jumbled up. It was like I wanted to be alone, but I didn't. I wanted to talk, but I didn't. I wanted to know what was going to happen next, but I didn't. I wanted to rewind time to back before this puberty business started. Or maybe I wanted to fast-forward until it was done, and I was all grown up and knew everything like Mom did.

Well, actually, the more I thought about it, I kind of did want to talk. But not to Mom.

I wanted to talk to Zoe.

Everything important that had ever happened to me had happened to her first. And that's how I liked it.

"Hey . . . Mom?" I asked as she pulled into our driveway.

"Yes?" she said, all eager. "What is it?"

"Can I . . . call Zoe?"

"Oh," Mom said. "Sure. Of course."

It wasn't until I was all by myself in my room, with Mom's phone tight in my hand, that I felt like I could take a deep breath. Luckily, I remembered to call Zoe's phone and not Aunt Rachel's. She answered on the first ring.

"Hi, Aunt Beth," Zoe said.

"It's me!"

"Abbyyyyy!" Zoe shrieked. She sounded really, truly happy to hear from me, which made me feel better already. "What's up?"

"I just got home from the doctor," I told her.

"Uh-oh. What's wrong? Are you sick or something? Did you get a shot?" she asked.

"Nope. No shots," I said, my heart going *thud-a-thud*. "So this is maybe weird, but . . . I noticed something the other day."

"What's that?" Zoe asked.

Then I told her about my bumps. "You can't even really see them, but I can definitely feel them," I told her. "Is that what it was like for you when you got them?"

There was a long pause. "Bumps where?" Zoe asked. "Like goosebumps?"

"No. Like . . . on my chest," I said.

"Bumps on your chest?" she repeated.

"Yeah. My . . . future breasts," I said, and then I burst out laughing. I mean, it was so funny! It was practically hilarious!

"I can't even tell if you're serious?" Zoe said, far away in California.

That's when I realized that talking on the phone was not enough. Not even close. If Zoe could see my face, she'd know I was serious. She'd know how much I needed to hear that there was nothing to feel weird about, that it had already happened to her, and everything was just fine.

"Pretty serious," I said. "Actually, completely serious."

There was a long, cringey silence while I waited for Zoe to say something. Anything. I'm not going to lie, it was rough.

When it was finally, painfully clear that she wasn't going to say anything, I changed the subject, fast. "Soooo . . . what's new with you?"

"I, um, met a new gymnastics coach," she said. "But I'm not sure I want to do gymnastics anymore. I'm not sure it's my thing."

"Oh? How come?"

"Abby," Mom said.

I spun around. When had she come into my room? Without knocking? And now she was just standing there like it was nothing? "I'm still on the phone!" I hissed.

Mom shot me a look. "I *know*," she said. "*My* phone. And I need to call Mr. Tucker. He's emailed me four times since I left work early."

The part she didn't say—*because of you and your appointment*—hung in the air.

"I have to go," I mumbled into the phone while Mom stood there with her hand out. "Talk to you later."

"Bye!" Zoe chirped.

I said bye, too, but I don't know if she heard me.

CHAPTER
5

That weekend, Mom had to go to work for a few hours. On a Saturday! We didn't get to go out to eat at The Breakfast Place or take a family bike ride or anything because Dad needed to catch up on all the chores that didn't get done during the week. I decided that Mr. Taylor, Mr. Taylor, and Mr. Tucker were just about as bad as Mr. Smiley.

After Mom left, though, I noticed something new on my dresser. It was a plastic tube with a flowery purple label that read JUST FOR TEENS! DEODORANT * SPRING MEADOW SCENT. *Huh?* I wondered. I wasn't a teen yet. Not even close!

The girl on the label was holding a finger to her lips, like she was whispering *Shhh!* or about to tell someone a big, juicy secret. I unscrewed the top and sniffed the rolly ball inside. It smelled like a bunch of flowers.

Then I heard a knock on the door. "Laundry delivery, pumpkin spice," Dad called out.

I scrambled up to open the door for him. Dad wasn't just carrying the laundry basket of clean clothes, though. He also had a big cardboard box under his arm.

"Pumpkin spice?" I repeated, giving Dad a *look*.

"No?" he asked. "I guess it *is* pretty seasonal. What can I say? I'm excited for fall."

"Listen," I said. "I don't mind if you call me 'princess.' I don't even know why I said that."

"Really?" Dad asked. "I'm enjoying the challenge of finding a new nickname for you."

"Okay, I guess. If you want," I replied. "What's in the box?"

"Mom ordered some stuff for Run Wild!" he said. "When does that start?"

"Monday," I groaned. "Don't remind me. Unless"—I looked up hopefully—"I can convince you to let me deliver packages again?"

"Sorry," Dad said, shaking his head. "Our decision is final. You should be doing fun after-school things like clubs, not tagging along on my work route."

Running? Fun? I thought. *Yeah, right!*

"But look on the bright side," Dad continued. "You love opening packages!"

That was true.

I pulled a long strip of tape off the box and dumped everything out. The first thing I noticed was a stack of books—the same ones that Dr. Camfield had recommended. Yeesh! I didn't want Dad to see them, so I sort of shoved them behind me, under my bed.

Besides the books, there was a blue duffel bag and swishy running shorts and tons of little things—a travel-size hairbrush, and a travel-size deodorant, and a little tin full of hair elastics. All the tiny travel-size stuff did look pretty cute. It would be even better if it were for taking a real trip. If only I could *run away* instead of Run Wild!

Then I scrunched up my face into a frown. "What are these? Baby wipes?" I asked, holding up a packet. There was no way I was bringing *baby wipes* to school, like I was some kind of baby or something.

Dad glanced at the packet. "Oh. Those are wash-and-go wipes," he said. "Not for babies."

"What are they for?"

"They're, like, washing-up wipes," he explained. "In case you feel like you're really sweaty, you won't have to clean off with bathroom soap."

My eyes went panic-wide. Did Mom tell him about my sweat problems?

Dad cleared his throat. "So . . . just so you know . . . ," he began.

Oh no, did she tell him about my *bumps*?

"You shouldn't feel bad about, ah, having body odor," Dad told me. "It's normal and natural."

I shrugged and looked away. "A lot of things that are normal and natural are also pretty gross," I replied.

"Maybe so, but you're not," he said. "And I know a lot of this stuff you'll want to talk to Mom about . . . but don't forget about your old dad, okay? I'm here for you, too."

"Thanks," I mumbled. Don't get me wrong. I was grateful. But I was also desperate to change the subject to, well, anything. Anything at all.

Dad grinned at me. Then he turned the laundry basket over and dumped my clothes out onto my bed!

"Whoa—what are you doing!" I exclaimed.

"I think you're old enough to fold your own laundry," he replied, still grinning. "And it would be a big help if you could do a few more chores around here, now that Mom and I are both working."

Ratzit, I thought. As if Run Wild! wasn't bad enough, now I had extra chores?

But I guess Dad had extra stuff to do, too, since Mom had to work so much, even on the weekends. So I sighed and said, "Sure. Fine."

"Thanks, kiddo," Dad said, giving me a kiss on the forehead. He started showing me how to fold shirts and stuff. Even though it was more boring than dirt, I tried to pay attention. Sort of. Well, not really.

Just as he was about to leave, I said, "Hey, Dad?"

"Yeah?" he asked.

"Can I use your phone to call Zoe?"

Dad glanced at the time on his phone and shook his head. "It's only seven a.m. there. Too early."

"Okay." I sighed.

"Sorry . . . buttercup," he replied.

"Buttercup?" I repeated, scrunching up my nose.

"Yeah, I'm not feeling it, either," Dad said. "Back to the drawing board."

After Dad left I stared at the pile of laundry. Folding it was the last thing I wanted to do. *It's just clothes,* I told myself. *Who cares if they get folded or not? I don't.*

I scooped up the pile of clothes and shoved it into my dresser. Then I grabbed my stationery set. If I couldn't talk to Zoe right this minute, writing to her would be the next best thing.

Hey Z!

How's California? Is it hot like summer there, because it is H-O-T here. Even the leaves are confused. They haven't started changing at all yet, but the pool is closed for the season, so you know summer is really over. So, this is funny. I have deodorant now! It's called "Spring Meadow" and smells like flowery soap or something. Do you have deodorant? What does it smell like? I miss you so much. Every day I have so much I want to tell you. More stuff than I could ever put in a letter. Anyway, write back soon! I want to hear everything—EVERYTHING!

I drew a row of hearts, and I colored each one in so that they looked like a rainbow. Then I signed a big letter *A* with a lot of swirly loops. And for the envelope I wrote Zoe's name and address as neatly and clearly as I could. I bet Mr. Smiley would have been impressed.

I pressed the stamp on hard to make sure it wouldn't fall off. Then I whispered, "Fly fast, flamingos!" I know it was dumb, but I couldn't wait for Zoe to get my letter.

Then, hopefully, she would remember to write back.

❋   ❋   ❋

Monday got off to a bad start. A *really* bad start. Not even my new duffel bag full of cool stuff for Run Wild! could make the jumpy jitters in my stomach go away. Things only got worse when I went to the kitchen for breakfast.

"Abby!" Mom exclaimed, frowning. "Why are your clothes so wrinkled?"

No *Good morning*, even.

I looked down at my T-shirt and skirt. Now that she mentioned it, they did look really crumpled. *Ugh*, I thought. *Maybe I should have folded them like Dad said.*

"Did you sleep in them?" asked Max. Like he should talk, with a big smear of jam on his chin.

"Shut up, Max," I mumbled, pulling and pressing at my clothes. It didn't help.

"Hey," Mom said, frowning more. "Don't say *shut up*. And I asked you a question."

I shrugged as I poured some cereal into a bowl. Some of it spilled onto the counter, which made me mad. "Who cares?"

"I care!" Mom said.

And, the truth was, I kind of cared, too, now that my clothes looked so messy.

"Abby, you were supposed to fold your clothes before you put them away," Dad reminded me.

"Okay! Sorry! I got it!" I said. I shoved the rest of my cereal in my mouth. "Can we go now?"

Then I banged out the door fast . . . completely forgetting to grab my brand-new duffel bag. I didn't realize I'd left it at home until the last bell rang and it was time to change for Run Wild! Of course.

Ratzit! I thought. Mom and Dad were both working this afternoon. There was no way I could go to the office and call them to bring it to me. I had no choice but to run in my school clothes and not my exercising clothes. I grabbed the edge of my skirt and pulled it down awkwardly as I hurried toward the field. I didn't want to make things even worse by being late on the first day of practice.

I'd seen Coach Wilde around school plenty of times. She was in charge of the early bird program for kids who ate breakfast at school, and she was a cafeteria monitor, and sometimes she was even a substitute teacher. Coach Wilde had this puffy, fluffy hair that was always, always pulled into a high ponytail that made her look even taller. Her entire wardrobe was tracksuits, the kind that went *swish-swish* whenever she moved, and she wore a silver whistle on a chain around her neck. She wasn't supposed to blow it inside— at least, that was the rumor—but if kids got rowdy in the cafeteria, look out! The whistle would go *wheeeeeeeeeeeeet- wheeeeeeeeeeeeeeeeeeeet!* until your ears were ready to bleed!

It won't all be running, I tried to tell myself. *There will have to be, like, warm-ups and cooldowns and stretching and—and—and—*

I didn't even know what else. But nobody could expect us to run for the whole two hours. Right?

It wasn't hard to find the Run Wild! crew. For starters, there were like forty kids in the middle of the field, and Coach Wilde's floofy ponytail stood out above them all. And her whistle was already working overtime, like it had been cooped up all day and was ready to be free. *Wheet-wheet-wheeeeeeeeeeet!*

This is not my scene, I thought with dread. Why couldn't I be in the drawing club? Or the library club? Or the kitten cuddling club? Hmm, if that last one didn't exist, maybe I could start it. We could—

Wheeeeeet! "Are all the newbies ready to join us?"

I jumped as all forty heads—that's eighty eyeballs, if you're mathing it—turned to stare at me. Coach Wilde hadn't exactly called me out by name, but I was sure everyone knew exactly who she was talking about. I hurried over to the group, cringing with every step as I realized how badly I stood out. Everyone else was wearing shorts or leggings or swishy pants. My skirt with the butterflies embroidered on it suddenly felt stiffer than ever. Maybe nobody would notice . . . I hoped.

Just then, Maya from Mr. Smiley's class ran up to me. I was so relieved to see a friend that I almost gave her a big hug before I remembered to be cool.

"Hey, Abby!" she said. "I didn't know you were into running!"

"I'm not—I mean, I'm new," I said. "New to Run Wild!"

"Very cool!" Then Maya pointed at my skirt. "Did you bring a change of clothes?"

"No," I said. "I forgot—"

"No problem," she said. "All the girls meet up in the bathroom by the gym, actually, and change right after school. You should come tomorrow. It's fun; we all get ready together."

Wheeeeeeeeet!

That whistle made everybody jump to attention.

"Welcome to Run Wild!" Coach Wilde announced. She was so *excited* to be there. I wished she could use her whistle to blow some of that enthusiasm my way. "Over the next few months, we're going to play, we're going to run, and most of all, we're going to have fun."

Does not compute, I thought in a robot voice. If Zoe was with me, I would have muttered it under my breath and watched her cheeks turn red as she tried not to laugh. I didn't know if Maya would laugh or just think I was a weirdo. So I kept my mouth shut.

"And by building our *speed*, our *strength*, and our *endurance*, we're going to train for the Wonder Run!"

Everybody was cheering, so I started clapping, too.

"The theme this year is Home for the Holidays," Coach Wilde continued.

Holidays. Somehow, I hadn't even thought about the holidays without Zoe and her family. Who would trick-or-treat with me? Max? No thank you! And what about Thanksgiving? Aunt Rachel cooked every year. And Christmas—nope. I pushed the thought right out of my head. If only Zoe could be home for the holidays . . .

Quit it, I said to myself in a mad way. Zoe *would* be home for the holidays. Because for her, home was California.

"By the time December rolls around, each and every one of you will be ready for the Wonder Run Five K—even our newbies," Coach Wilde was saying. "But you don't have to worry about that yet—"

Good, I thought, because I didn't even know what a 5K was. And I wasn't sure I wanted to find out.

"—because today, we're going to start with the basics. First things first—a warm-up run!"

I took a deep breath. It was not a good sign if even the warm-ups involved running.

Whoosh! Suddenly, everyone was running, so I joined in the pack, too. Some kids—the really fast ones—zipped right to the front, while the slower ones fell farther and farther behind. Most of us, though, were right smack in the middle. Coach Wilde seemed to be everywhere—front, middle, back—yelling encouraging things like "You can do it!" and "I believe in you!" as we looped around the field.

By the time we got back to the benches, I was way out of breath. But we were just getting started. Next came ten push-ups. My arms were wobbly after three, so I stood up and tried to look like I'd finished already. Then we did a drill called karaoke, but nobody did any singing. Instead, we traveled sideways along the field with our feet crisscrossing. My big triumph was not falling flat on my face. The best part was when Coach Wilde told us to skip. Just skip—in lines, in loops, wherever we wanted. Skipping—now *that* was something I could handle. After all, Zoe taught me how to skip back when we were in preschool. My skirt was a problem, though. Somehow it was stiff enough that I couldn't stretch my legs all the way to run—but threatened to flounce and bounce around with any big movements. I had to keep my arms kind of pinned to my sides so that my skirt wouldn't whoosh up. Hopefully, I didn't look as silly as I felt . . . but I probably did.

By the time Run Wild! ended, I was totally worn out. Now when I dragged my feet across the field, it was because my muscles were so mad at me, they didn't want to move anymore. Not one inch.

But I could see Mom's car at the curb. Inside that car was Mom and my escape home. I wanted them both—Mom *and* home—more than anything right now.

The instant I got into the car, Mom turned around to smile at me. "How was it?" she asked, all bright and sunshiny. The happiness in her voice twisted my relief at seeing her into something grumpy and grouchy. How could she be so happy when I was so miserable?

"Horrible," I said, sinking into my seat and buckling my seat belt like I was mad at it, too. "I hated it! And I didn't even have the right stuff!"

I snuck a glance in the rearview mirror, just long enough to see that Mom's smile was already gone. Now I felt even worse—and that made me angry. Why should *I* feel guilty when *she* was the one forcing me to do stupid running when everybody knows I hate running the most?

"What—what kind of stuff do you need?" she asked. "I thought I ordered everything . . ."

I pressed my lips together, stared out the window, and refused to say another word. It was *my* fault I didn't have my duffel bag, just like it was *my* fault my clothes were all wrinkled, but the last thing I needed was to hear Mom say that.

Plus, I was saving all my words for Zoe.

Hey Z,

Well, I did it. I survived the first day of Run Wild! That's the good news. The bad news is that it's only going to get worse from here. We are training to run in a 5K. The K stands for *kilometers*, and since we have to run FIVE of them—count them: one-two-three-four-five—that's actually going to be 3.1 miles. MILES! Dad looked it up on his phone. I already know I won't make it to the end. I might not even make it to the end of the next Run Wild! practice.

Well, enough complaining. Are you doing any after-school activities? I was thinking, if gymnastics isn't your thing anymore, maybe you could join a baking club! Or be on a baking show? You know, I haven't even had a cupcake since your goodbye party because yours are the BEST. Oh! I almost forgot—how's your pool?!?! Do you swim every day?

I hope you write back soon! If you are too busy during the daytime, maybe you could write to me at night, with a flashlight, when you are supposed to be asleep. Just an idea!

Love,

A

CHAPTER 6

All of a sudden it was October, which meant so many awesome things: Halloween and pumpkins and toasting marshmallows around the firepit in the backyard. I wondered what Mrs. Flamingo was going to do with her flamingos for Halloween. Last year, she dressed them up in pointy witch hats and arranged them around a big black cauldron in the middle of her yard. Then, on Halloween night, she filled the cauldron up to the brim with candy!

I wondered if Daphne helped her aunt with the flamingos. And if she was still living in her car.

The cooler weather meant I could start wearing my sweaters without sweating like crazy. I still put deodorant on every day, though—just in case. Especially because things were getting more intense. Not just with Run Wild! but with fourth grade, too.

We had barely finished listening to morning announcements one day when Mr. Smiley walked over to the SMART Board. "Who knows what today is?" he asked, gesturing at the calendar.

"Uh . . . Wednesday?" Garrett said.

"And?" Mr. Smiley prompted.

"The second?" Savannah guessed.

"*And?*" Mr. Smiley repeated.

He obviously knew the answer. Why wouldn't he just tell us?

"It's been more than one month since the first day of school," Mr. Smiley said. "That means it's time to get down to business."

I glanced over at Maya, who was already looking at me. She seemed as confused as I felt. What was Mr. Smiley even talking about? We'd already been working really hard!

"On the first day of school, I mentioned a geography bee," he continued. "In this competition next spring, you'll be quizzed on your knowledge of current events, global history, and the world's geography. One way we'll be preparing is by studying maps. Why are maps important?"

There was total silence. It seemed kind of like a trick question.

"For . . . going places?" Reese asked.

"That's one reason," Mr. Smiley said. "Maps help us find our way. They can show us where we are . . . where we're going . . . and how to get home again. Maps can also help us understand our history."

Mr. Smiley crossed the room and stood between two maps on the wall. "Take these maps of the world, for example," he said. "They were created five hundred years apart. This one, over here, was entirely drawn by hand. If you take a close look, you can see that the continents are misshapen. The scales and proportions are completely off. Even some of the countries' names—and borders—have changed over the centuries. Now, this map is from last year. Cartographers used images from space and computers to create the most precise map of the planet in history."

Wow, I thought. Was anyone else as surprised as I was by how cool maps were? I couldn't tell, so I kept my face blank like everybody else.

Next to me, Maya raised her hand. "What's a cartographer?" she asked.

"A cartographer is someone who makes maps," Mr. Smiley explained. "With this assignment you're all going to become cartographers."

There it was. There was *always* a catch—and it usually meant more work!

"We're going to learn about direction, scale, perspective, symbols," Mr. Smiley said, ticking each one off on his fingers. "When we finish this unit, you'll be able to read any map you come across."

Leo raised his hand. "Isn't it just easier to use GPS?"

The corners of Mr. Smiley's mouth twitched, and for half a second, I thought he might smile, but nope. "Not if you lose your phone or it runs out of battery," he said. "What would you do if you were lost in the middle of the desert and couldn't get a signal?"

Well, when you put it like that . . . I thought.

Mr. Smiley reached under his desk and pulled out a big box. I sat up a little straighter. There was a rustling through the room, even a little whispering, as we all wondered, *What's in there?*

The big reveal was disappointing for most people, but not me. I mean, I wasn't so interested in the rulers and pro-tractors and silver compasses that he passed out, but Mr. Smiley's box *also* had a stack of bright-white, heavy artist paper—the kind you could use with permanent markers or watercolors, or both.

"Your project, which will be due in early December, is to make a map," Mr. Smiley said. "You can use any supplies you want, but it must be done *neatly*, so you'll need to turn in a rough draft before you have approval to create the final version on this special paper."

Maya raised her hand again. "A map of where?" she asked.

"It should be a place that's special to you," Mr. Smiley said. "It could be your neighborhood. It could be your favor-ite vacation spot, or a country you can't wait to visit some-day. It could be school—"

In the back, someone snort-laughed, which made Mr. Smiley scowl.

But I was smiling. Grinning, even. I could already tell this wasn't just a geography project. It was also an art project—and that meant I couldn't wait to get started!

✾　✾　✾

No lie, if I didn't have Run Wild!, I would've gotten started on my map right after school. Instead, Maya and I went to the bathroom to get ready. If we changed into our running gear fast enough, there was usually enough time for her to braid my hair. She did a great job, weaving up all the wispy bits so they wouldn't escape, no matter how much I ran around.

My feet were pretty draggy as we went out to the field, but I didn't want to make Maya late, so I tried to keep up. Coach Wilde was blowing her whistle. *Wheeeeeeeeeeeeet, wheeeeeeeeeeeeeet, wheeeeeeeeeeeeeeeeeeeeeeeeeeeeeeeeeeeet!*

"We're going to do something a little different today, Wild Runners," Coach announced as we gathered around her. "Fast track warm-ups!"

I glanced at Maya and mouthed, "Huh?" But she just grinned back.

"There are different stations around the field," Coach continued. "You'll have ninety seconds to complete each one. It doesn't matter where you start as long as you cycle through all of them. When you hear the whistle, it's time to move to the next station. Got it?"

"Got it!" we yelled.

"One—two—" *Wheeeeeeeeeeeeeeeeeeeeeeeeet!*

Everybody was screaming and laughing as we ran around the field to the different stations. There was one with hoops on the ground, which we had to hop through lightly on the tips of our toes. There was a station with cones you had to run around in big, twisty loops. There was another one for push-ups—*gag barf blech*. There was a station for karaoke, and a jump rope station and a lap-around-the-track station. Maya and I stuck together and zipped from station to station, always finishing just as Coach Wilde's whistle wheeted.

"Where next?" I panted when we finished up the jump rope station.

"That's it," Maya said, stretching her arms over her head. "We did all the stations!" She wasn't even a little bit out of breath, which was pretty incredible. This was her third year of Run Wild! Maybe if I did it for three years, but nope. I was going to switch to a new after-school activity in January.

"Charlieeee! Charlieeee! Charlieeee!"

I turned around when I heard voices chanting Charlie's name. "What's going on?" I asked.

Maya pointed to where Charlie was just getting started at the big run around the track.

"Is he still warming up?" I asked. "I thought warm-ups were over."

"They are," Maya said. "But Charlie didn't finish, so . . ."

It felt like a magnet was pulling Maya and me across the field. We joined the other runners, and the next thing I knew, we were all running behind Charlie. Slow—slower than me, even—but steady, and chanting his name. Not in a ha-ha-Charlie's-a-slowpoke way. But in an upbeat, encouraging, you-got-this! way. I knew that if Charlie slowed down, we would, too. If he fell, we would pick him up. We were there for him—like, literally right there for him, right behind him all the way. We kept chanting his name, slowly at first, and then faster and faster and louder and louder until, when he reached the end of the track, we were screaming it.

"Charlieeeeeeeeeeeeeeeeeeeeeeeeee!"

He doubled over, hands on his knees, face red and sweaty, with his hair all stuck to his forehead. He was too out of breath to talk.

But the grin on his face as we gathered around, slapping his back and clapping our hands, said everything.

"Let's keep the challenges coming, runners!" Coach Wilde announced. "Drumroll, please . . ."

As soon as everyone was smacking their thighs to provide the sound effect, Coach Wilde grinned and said, "Relay races! Now, grab a partner and form groups of four—"

That was the exact moment I shut down. I already knew that nobody would want to be my partner. I just *knew* it, and there was nothing I could do to stop it. I'd just have to stand here and pretend that I didn't care. Maya had been doing Run Wild! for years; no doubt she already had a favorite partner, of course. Probably everybody did.

"Abby!"

I turned around and saw Maya calling for me. She was standing with Leah and Lucy. As they waved me over, I couldn't believe it, but it was true—they wanted me to join their group! I walked up to them like it was no big deal, but if they had mind-reading powers, they would've seen how my brain was practically throwing a party, with confetti and balloons and everything.

"Remember how we've been practicing skipping?" Coach Wilde was saying. "Well, here's a little secret: Skipping is just running in slow motion!"

No way, I thought.

But Coach Wilde was already demonstrating, with big, swoopy, exaggerated motions that made everybody crack up. I tilted my head to the side a little as I thought about it. Skipping wasn't so bad. I mean, even I could skip. So if Coach Wilde was right, maybe I wouldn't make a giant fool of myself during the relay race. Maybe.

"Want me to start?" Maya asked.

"Sure," I said. So Maya jogged over to the starting line, while I waited for her at the start of the second leg.

Wheeeeet!

The starting runners took off! My muscles got tingly, like they were being hit with little zaps of electricity, as I watched Maya approach. I had to be ready to take the baton and start running at the same time. I didn't want to mess it up—for Maya or me or anyone on our team.

Then Maya was right behind me. For less than a moment, the baton was in her hand and mine.

Then it was just in mine.

It was time to run!

I stared straight ahead and remembered what to do: skipping, but speedy. *This isn't so bad,* I thought as my feet went *thud-thud! Thud-thud! Thud-thud!* My body was this awesome machine—all the different parts doing their own thing, but also working together, the way my arms and legs were moving in an opposite but perfect pattern. Left foot *down*, right arm *forward*, right foot *down*, left arm *forward*, over and over and over, and suddenly, I didn't feel like I was running.

I felt like I was flying!

For, like, half a second.

Then: *Splat!*

That wasn't supposed to happen. I didn't even know *what* happened until I found myself in a sunken spot in the field, a tangle of arms and legs. My thoughts pounded through my brain as I realized that I had tripped like a big idiot, right in front of everybody. *Get up!* my brain yelled at me. *Get up and walk it off!*

Coach's whistle was wheeting away.

"Ha-ha! I'm fine!" I said, forcing a laugh.

Then I tried to take a step and immediately crumpled back down to the ground.

It seemed my foot did not agree with me. It was throbbing now, too, hurting bad enough that tears sprang to my eyes. A new thought pulsed through my brain: *Don't cry, don't cry, don't cry . . .*

"Hey, hey," Coach Wilde was saying. How'd she gotten to me so fast? Oh, right. Running. She wasn't the only one. Maya was there, looking worried, and Leah and Lucy, too. I guess I'd pretty much disqualified our whole team.

"I'm sorry," I said. It was automatic.

"No need for that," Coach Wilde said. Then she pulled me up—she was so strong and so gentle at the same time, more opposites working together in ways I didn't expect—and helped me limp-hop over to the bench.

"Where does it hurt? Let's see," she said.

My hands were a little shaky as I took off my sneaker.

"What's that smell? It smells like feet," Leah said.

It was me, of course. After all, I was the only one with my shoe off. If faces could burst into flames, I think mine would've. *Is every part of me destined to be stinky?* I wondered.

"That's just sweat," Coach Wilde said. She didn't look up from my smelly foot or flinch or anything. "I like the smell of sweat. It means somebody has been moving their body and that they really mean it."

If Zoe were here, we would have shared one of our special looks. Why was I surprised that Coach Wilde likes the smell of sweat? That was just her trademark brand of weird.

Coach gently peeled off my damp sock and cradled my foot in her hand. "Right here," she said, her index finger hovering over my pinkie toe, which had already swelled to the size of a cocktail wiener. "Bet you dollars to doughnuts that it's broken."

"What does that mean?" I cried. I meant about it being broken, but also the dollars-to-doughnuts part. What was she even talking about? What did dollars have to do with anything? Or doughnuts?

Coach Wilde finally glanced up. "It means," she said, "that I'm calling your parents, and practice is over. For you, anyway."

❄ ❄ ❄

Mom couldn't leave work, even though I wanted her so bad—the way I always wanted her when I was sick or hurt or when things spiraled off into Disaster-ville. By the time Dad picked me up from school, my foot was too swollen to squeeze back into my sneaker. He helped me hobble out to the car. While he drove I snuck one of those shower-wipe-thingies out of my duffel and swiped it over my foot. That way I wouldn't stink up the doctor's office, too.

Everything was like déjà vu, which is what you say when you feel like you've already done something before, but this time I didn't kick the table at all. I figured my feet had been through enough already.

"Abby McAdams, we meet again," Dr. Camfield said. "Now, I love the color blue, but not on toes."

I laughed a little, even though my bruised-up foot was hurting more every second.

"How did this happen?" she asked.

I explained about the relay race. Then I added something extra. "I fall a lot, actually. Not just during sports. Sometimes I even fall over my own feet. Just call me Abby McAdams, Super Klutz."

I was trying to make a joke, but Dr. Camfield didn't laugh. "I bet your feet have grown a lot lately," she said.

"They did during the summer," I said. "I got new sandals, and then in like a month, my toes were curling over the edge, and I had to get even bigger sandals."

"Hands and feet undergo a rapid growth spurt at the start of puberty," Dr. Camfield said. "It can take a while for the rest of your body to catch up."

My hands? I thought. I held them up. Maybe they were looking kind of big.

"So that's why many girls your age trip and stumble a lot," she continued. "You're not a klutz. You're just getting used to taking up space in a different way. Now, I'm going to send you off for an X-ray of your foot, and then we'll figure out what to do next."

Dad couldn't come with me for the X-ray part, but I tried to be brave, even though the machine was huge and freaky-looking. It was cool to see a picture of my bones. That's how we found out that I had not one but *two* broken toes! Dr. Camfield told me that there are twenty-six bones in my foot, and I broke two of them. I was kind of excited, actually. Two broken toes were a much bigger deal than just one.

"The good news is that they're hairline fractures," Dr. Camfield was telling Dad. "Very clean; we almost can't even see them on the X-ray. They should heal nice and quick—probably before Halloween. Hear that, Abby? You won't even need a cast!"

"I won't?" I asked. That was a major disappointment. I'd always wanted to get a cast, but not even breaking *two different bones* could make my dream come true.

"Nope!" Dr. Camfield said brightly. "You will need to wear a special boot, though. Let me see if we have your size."

That didn't sound so bad. Boots are pretty cool. But what Dr. Camfield brought back was the opposite of cool. It was a clunky black thing with wide Velcro straps.

"It's your lucky day, Abby," she said. "We have one left!"

"Just one?" I asked. "But I have two feet."

"It's a medical boot, Abby, and it's for your injured foot," Dad told me. "You can wear a regular shoe on your other foot."

I squeezed my eyes shut in horror as I imagined myself hobbling around school with a regular shoe on one foot and a boot that looked like a lumpy trash bag on the other. Now, that was going to look great. Just great!

I didn't say much as Dr. Camfield showed Dad how to tape my broken toes to the next one that wasn't broken. "It's called 'buddy taping,'" she explained. "The healthy toe will support the other two as they heal. Like a real buddy!"

It was great that my broken toes had a buddy to help them out. Suddenly, Maya popped into my head. We'd become really good friends spending so many afternoons in Run Wild! together.

What would happen now that I couldn't run with her anymore?

CHAPTER 7

The sun was just starting to set as Dad and I left Dr. Camfield's office to pick up Max. Inside the clunky black boot, my toes were hurting worse than before—a weird throbby pain that I could almost feel in my stomach, too. Dad helped me get into the car, and if I'm totally honest, I leaned against him a lot. Maybe even more than I needed to.

I stared out the window as Dad drove through Winston-Salem. We were getting closer to downtown and some of my favorite places—Bookmarks and Penny Lane Café and the Emporium Theater. There had been a lot of construction over the past couple years. Sometimes, on pretty days, Mom would bring Max and me to watch all the construction vehicles. Back before she went to work, I mean.

Now those dusty sites had been transformed into tall, sleek buildings with huge windows and perfect little plants out front. One of them had a sign that read LUXURY LIVING IN THE HEART OF THE CITY.

I knew what luxury meant. Things like gold plates and fancy jewelry and private jets. Out of nowhere, I thought about Daphne's rusty car as I stared at the shiny building with silver trim, and something didn't make sense.

Then, on the corner, I saw something else: a person hunched over a shopping cart that was as jam-packed as Daphne's car. Instead of grocery bags, there was lots of random stuff—books and newspapers and cans and I don't even know what else. It looked like junk. Or trash.

Even though the car windows were closed, I could hear the grocery cart's wheels squeeeeaking as the person slowly pushed it along. They didn't have real shoes on but rather old sandals, one with a broken strap that slapped against the pavement. There were cars in the streets, and people hurrying down the sidewalk, and nobody looked at the person. Nobody even noticed them.

Except, maybe, for me.

The light changed, and Dad drove forward.

"Wait," I said.

"What's up?" he asked.

"Wait!"

Dad stepped on the brake hard, but my seat belt kept me from flying forward. "What's wrong, Abby? Is it your foot?"

"That person—with the cart—"

But they were already gone.

A wave of whooshiness swelled in my stomach as Dad started driving again. I leaned back, closed my eyes, and tried to take a deep breath. It had been a couple years since the last time I got carsick, and I didn't *think* I was going to throw up, but I definitely felt very, very bad—and it wasn't just my toes.

I was still in a terrible mood when we got home, and I wanted a Mom-hug so, so much, but she wasn't back from work. That stung like getting a shot. I had *two* broken toes, and she couldn't even leave a little early?

"How's your foot, Toes?" Dad asked, trying to be funny. I was *not* in the mood.

"It hurts. A lot," I snapped. "And don't call me 'Toes.'"

"Sorry," Dad replied. "Let's see if I can find some medicine for you."

I went straight to my room—*stomp*-step, *stomp*-step—down the hall. My house seemed so big all of a sudden. Too big. There were four bedrooms, one for Mom and Dad, one for Max, one for me, and one for when somebody comes to visit. Imagine! A whole bedroom, just sitting empty most of the time, with a bed and pillows and blankets and a dresser full of drawers with nothing in them. I bet Mrs. Flamingo's niece would have been plenty happy to sleep in that room instead of her car.

I even felt bad about my own room. My bed had four pillows and a giant fluffy blanket *and* a trundle bed tucked under it for when I had sleepovers.

The living room had a sleeper sofa that no one ever slept on.

The playroom had a futon.

Suddenly, my whole house was full of space and beds that nobody used. There was only one explanation I could think of: My whole family was full of bed hogs. And I don't mean the kind that roll over and take the covers with them.

It wasn't all the way dark yet, so I decided to go into the

backyard. I hadn't been out there much since I started doing Run Wild! The leaves on the maple tree had changed color, all red and orange like a blazing bonfire spreading through the branches. They had started to fall, too, and were drifting, one at a time, onto the roof of the playhouse that Dad built for me back when I was in preschool.

Playhouse.

A whole house, just for playing.

When was the last time I'd used it? Zoe and I used to hang out in there all the time and pretend we had cooked the picnic lunches Mom made us. That was a while ago, though.

I walked over and peeked in through the window. The playhouse was dusty inside, with cobwebs in the corners and a carpet of crunched-up dried leaves. But it was plenty big for an air mattress and a sleeping bag. Mrs. Flamingo's niece could have slept there, instead of her car.

Instead, it just sat empty. A waste of space.

The wrongness of it all kept swelling inside me, making me feel worse and worse as my foot hurt more and more. I hobble-stomped back into the house and looked everywhere for Max. He was watching TV with Pet in his lap and his mouth hanging open.

"Max," I said.

He was practically drooling. Ugh, gross!

"Max!" I yelled, stomping my good foot. "Pay attention! This is important!"

His eyes flicked over at me for half a second. "What?" he asked. But it was obvious he was still focused on his show.

"You need to go outside and play in that playhouse," I ordered him.

He didn't even answer me. Now I was so mad that I thought I was going to explode. I grabbed the remote and turned off the TV. And *then* I unplugged it!

Max let out such a howl that I kind of wanted to slap him. Or at least slap my hand over his mouth.

"You watch too much TV," I said, and pointed to the backyard. "Go outside and play in the playhouse right now!"

Max howled again, even louder, and this time it sounded like "*Mooooommmmmmmmmm!*"

His timing was perfect—better than mine ever was—because Mom came through the door just in time to hear the *ommmmmmm* part.

"What? What?" she asked, dashing into the living room, still carrying a pizza box. Max was crying now—I mean, come on—crying real tears! Mom looked at him, and at me, and I tried to hide the remote that was still in my hand, but it was too late.

"What's going on—" she began. "Abby—Oh, sweet pea, let's get you off your foot—"

"Abby broke the TV!" Max bawled.

I hated the way Mom looked at me, all surprised and disappointed.

"I did not!" I exclaimed. "But Max watches too much TV, and he never plays in the playhouse. It's so wasteful."

"BZZZZT! Wrong!" he hollered.

"Thank you, Abby, but I'm the mom here," she said. "Turn Max's show back on and go lie down, please. I'll get an ice pack for your toes."

I stared at her without moving a muscle.

"Abby. Turn. It. On," Mom said. Her words were all choppy and clipped, like she was too mad to even say them right.

I held up the remote with two fingers—just high enough that Max couldn't reach it. He started howling and leaping for it like some kind of maniac monkey.

"Abby!" Mom yelled. "Enough!"

I gave her another long stare. Just before she really lost her temper, I dropped the remote onto the floor and slowly stalked out of the room.

"Hey, kiddo," Dad said in the hall. But I pretended like I couldn't even see or hear him.

"What's going on?" I heard him ask.

"Where were you?" Mom said, still mad. "The kids were in a full-on brawl when I got home."

"They were?" He sounded surprised.

"I would like to come home from work and be able to take off my coat before breaking up World War III," Mom said.

"*I* was trying to find the children's Tylenol," Dad shot back. "Why are *you* late? I still have deliveries to make!"

Now the whole family was fighting, all because of me. Good. I didn't care. I slammed my door extra hard, that's how much I didn't care.

But that slam made the wall shudder, and my favorite picture of Zoe and me fell down. Not only did the glass break, but the corner of the frame chipped. Just like that, all the mad in me drained away like dirty bathwater and left me feeling soggy with sorrow. I wanted to cry—I had a crying–sore throat, even—but what was the point? It wouldn't help anything.

"Sorry," I whispered, to everyone and no one. Everything was wrong. Everything was unfair. I sat on the floor and started picking up the broken glass, extra careful so I wouldn't get cut, and that's when the tears started to slip down my cheeks.

There was a knock at the door, and Mom poked her head in before I said a word.

"Did I hear something br—" she began. Then she saw the broken glass and my tear-wet face and freaked out. "Abby! What happened? Are you hurt?"

I just shrugged. Besides my toes, I didn't have any hurts on the outside, but a great big one inside that was making me more miserable than I could even say.

Mom knelt down and took the broken glass out of my hands. Then she guided me over to the bed and sat next to me. I leaned my head on her shoulder and smelled her soft, warm Mom smell. It was so comfortable and safe that I cried harder.

Mom let me cry, stroking my hair as I got tears and snot

all over her pretty work blouse. She didn't seem to care about that, which made me cry even more.

"Shh, shh, shh," Mom said. "What happened, Abby? Is it your foot? Something at school?"

I shook my head and gulped and started telling her about Mrs. Flamingo's niece and the person with the shopping cart and the cobwebby playhouse. "And we have too many beds and sleeping places!" I finished, hiccupping. "Too many everythings!"

"Okay," Mom said, sighing. "I think I understand. But this is a big conversation, sweet pea. Bigger than we can have right now, with it getting late and everything. Let's go eat some dinner. I got a pizza and—"

Dinner. I hadn't even thought of that. If you live in a car, do you get to eat dinner? What if you only have a shopping cart? I opened my mouth wide and howled even louder than Max.

Mom rubbed her eyes, smearing black specks of mascara onto her cheeks. "Here's what's going to happen," she said in her no-messing-around voice. "Wash your face and come to the kitchen. Then we'll talk."

✳ ✳ ✳

I don't know how, but washing my face did make me feel better—a little bit. When I got to the kitchen, I realized that there were only three plates on the table.

"Where's Max?" I asked.

"He's going to eat dinner in front of the TV tonight," Mom said. "A special treat for him, and a chance for us to talk to you."

I sat down at the table and stared at my plate. Pizza, *again*, but I knew that wasn't why I'd lost my appetite. I poked at the cheese and wondered if Daphne had a pillow and blankets in her car. And if that other person had somewhere to sleep that was indoors. I liked camping once in a while, but not every night, and not when fall was here, and each night was colder than the one before.

Dad was looking closely at my face. "So," he began. "Mom got me up to speed. It sounds like you're upset about what we talked about in the car when we delivered packages? About homelessness and affordable housing?"

I nodded.

"It is upsetting," Dad continued. "To be honest, I'm glad that it's upset you. That's your humanity shining through, Abby. That's your heart."

"It's really wrong," I said, staring at my plate. "It's not fair that some people get to live in apartments and houses and have enough food while other people have nothing!"

"No," Mom said gently. "No, it's not fair."

"Then how come nobody's doing anything about it?" I asked, getting madder and madder. I stabbed my pizza with a fork, which wasn't really fair. It wasn't the pizza's fault.

"Who said nobody's doing anything?" Dad asked.

I looked up.

"There are homeless shelters, where people can sleep indoors instead of on the street," he began. "Soup kitchens and food pantries, where the hungry can get a meal. There are a lot of people trying to help. But it's a complicated problem, with many different causes, which makes it even more challenging to solve."

I hated it when Mom or Dad were right *and* making perfect sense. It actually made me even madder. "But they're not doing enough," I argued. "Nobody should be sleeping in a car or living out of a shopping cart! It's wrong! It's so wrong!"

"Actually, some people are working on a new approach to homelessness," Mom spoke up.

Dad and I looked at her.

"It's called 'a tiny-house community,'" she continued.

"A tiny house? Like the playhouse?" I asked.

"Yes and no," Mom replied. "The playhouse isn't a real house, Abby. You know that. It's not insulated, for example, so it won't stay warm enough in the winter. It doesn't have electricity or running water or a kitchen or a—"

"Okay, okay, I get it," I interrupted her. The more she talked, the worse I felt for yelling at Max about the playhouse.

"But a tiny house does have those things," Mom said. "It's small, so it needs a lot less land, and it's much less expensive to build. And the idea is that people who are homeless or struggling to afford a regular-size house can live in a tiny house and have a place to call home."

"We're going to have a tiny-house community here?" Dad asked.

Mom nodded. "Hopefully," she said. "There's a proposal going to the city council later this month. There's a pair of vacant lots for sale, but the zoning needs to change. And there are some fundraising efforts underway."

I stared at Mom, amazed. How did she know so much about it?

Mom must have understood my expression. She smiled and said, "Taylor, Taylor, and Tucker is donating legal services to the efforts," she explained.

"*You're* working on it?" I exclaimed.

"Unfortunately not," Mom said. "But I hear about it in the office. Mr. Taylor is very engaged in these efforts. In fact, it looks like the firm is going to be a major sponsor of the Wonder Run."

"Huh?" I asked. I remembered how Coach Wilde mentioned the Wonder Run at our very first practice, but what did that have to do with anything?

"The Wonder Run is a big fundraiser," Mom said. "Every year the money raised goes to a different charity. And this year—"

"Home for the Holidays!" I said, remembering the theme. Everything was starting to make sense now.

"Yes! Exactly," Mom said. "So, you see, there are a lot of people working on this problem, all of them trying to find different ways to help. Even if we don't always see their efforts."

"Okay," I said. "That's good to know."

And just like that, I was hungry. My pizza was kind of cold, but it tasted better than anything I'd ever eaten.

At bedtime I went over to Max's room. He was already in bed, waiting for Mom to come read him a book. Even from the doorway, I could tell he was all warm and snuggly in his pj's. I loved him the most right before bed, when he was sleepy and calm and quiet.

"I'm sorry, Max," I said.

He blinked at me, but he didn't say anything, so I could tell he was still upset.

"Hold on," I said. Then I dashed over to my room and got two shiny quarters out of my little red bank.

Back in Max's room, I held out the quarters. "Is Pet hungry? I brought him a snack," I said.

Max reached under his bed for Pet. Pet was getting pretty clinky with all that change in him.

I talked in a funny voice. "Yum, yum, I can't wait to eat up this money," I said, pretending to be Pet.

Max laughed, not a big laugh, but enough. "Please don't break the TV, Abby," he said.

"I didn't break it. I just unplugged—" I started to say. But his eyelids were already drooping, so instead, I said, "Okay. I won't. Good night, Max."

"Don't forget Pet," he mumbled, half asleep.

"Good night, Pet," I said. "Sweet dreams, you two."

Back in my room, I got out my flamingo paper. I stared at the page for a long minute before I started to write.

Hey Z,

How are you? What a day. I was—

I put down my pen and stared at the letter. There was so much to tell Zoe. Almost too much. More than could fit in a letter.

I guess Zoe had to be there. Or maybe what I meant was that she had to be *here*. So I crumpled up the half-written letter and threw it into the trash.

CHAPTER
8

The next morning Mom woke me up before my alarm. She was standing in the doorway, holding a mug of hot chocolate that had big pillowy marshmallows on top. "Morning, Abby," she said. "How's your foot feeling?"

I tried not to wiggle my broken toes, which were still taped together like some kind of mutant mega-toe. "Okay . . . I think. Is that cocoa?" I asked, scrunching my eyes up against the light.

She nodded. "It's full of calcium for your healing bones."

"I still wish I could've had a cast," I said. "You know they make them in all colors? And then everyone gets to write on it and draw little pictures?"

"Sorry, sweet pea," Mom replied. Then she held up her other hand and shook it back and forth. I heard a faint *clackety-clackety-clackety.* "But maybe this will help you feel better."

"Nail polish?" I guessed.

Mom nodded as she unfolded her fingers. "It's called 'unicorn,'" she said. "And it changes color depending on your body heat! Pretty cool, huh? I picked it up on the way home from work last night."

"Very cool," I said, staring at the shimmery polish. It was kind of a silvery purple, but from the cap I could tell that it would change color to blue and pink. Zoe would've loved it. Maybe I could send her some for Christmas.

"I'm sorry I couldn't take you to the doctor yesterday," Mom was saying. "You know how much I wanted to be there. But—"

"Let me guess." I sighed. "Taylor, Taylor, and Tucker."

Mom nodded. "Anyway, the least I can do is polish your little piggies."

I grinned. Mom hadn't called my toes "piggies" since I was small, but it still sounded as funny as it did back then. Somehow, it made me feel better about everything.

I tried to sit very still while Mom painted my toenails, only moving to sip my cocoa. When she finished, she stood up and said, "Okay. Hang out for ten or fifteen minutes to let the polish dry. Do you need anything before I go wake up Max?"

I pointed to my desk. "Can you hand me my flamingo stationery?" I asked.

Suddenly, I knew exactly what to write to Zoe. I didn't have to tell her *every* single thing that happened, like how bad I felt about homelessness. Or the fact that my terrible mood started a big family fight. I could just write the easy stuff.

✽   ✽   ✽

Dear Z,

You will never believe what I did at Run Wild! I fell in a hole on the field and broke my toes! That's right, toeS as in TWO. Which is ⅕ or 20% of my toes! We are doing fractions now, and Mr. Smiley is right: You can find them everywhere if you look.

You would laugh so hard if you could see the HIDEOUSLY UGLY boot-thing I have to wear for the next three weeks. If I had a phone, I would text you a picture, but I'll just have to draw you one instead. It is so gross. Just think, some doctor somewhere thought this would be better than a cast! What a meanie.

The good news is that I won't have to Run Wild! for three weeks. Or . . . maybe even longer, if my toes take a long, long, loooong time to heal. The longer it takes, the less I have to run!

I'm not sure if you got my other letters. I hope so. Please write back so I know for sure. I miss you the mostest.

Love,

A

After school each day, I brought my backpack instead of my duffel bag to the field. I figured I could get my homework done during Run Wild! practice, but it was hard to concentrate. Every time Coach went *wheeeeeeeeeeeet!* I wanted to see what was up.

Then something weird happened—really weird. I was watching the relay race, and I suddenly wanted to be out on the field, running with my teammates. Maya and Leah and Lucy had picked me, and as I watched them try to complete the race with just three people, I knew I'd let them down.

Can't wait to say goodbye to you, I thought, staring at my boot. It was true for a lot of reasons. The one I didn't expect, though, was that I wanted to be back on the field. Not for all of it. Definitely not for push-ups.

But skipping was pretty fun, and so was the karaoke drill. Even running relays with Maya, Leah, and Lucy was better than pretending to do homework on the bench.

I abandoned my homework and started drawing for fun instead, a picture of cats running a relay race. It was a funny picture because the cats were all wearing sneakers on their paws. That's a lot of shoes!

"I like the high-tops," Coach Wilde said, pointing at my drawing.

I jumped and slapped my hand over my notebook, a total reflex. I'd been so focused on my drawing that I didn't notice when Coach Wilde sat down next to me. She could be pretty quiet when she wasn't blowing her whistle.

"I heard you were a good artist," she continued.

"You did?" I said, surprised.

Coach nodded. "Mr. Smiley told me he's been observing your work in class and your map project is one of the best he's ever seen," she replied.

I nearly fell off the bench.

"So I was wondering," she said. "How would you like to draw the picture for the Wonder Run posters and T-shirts?"

I stared at Coach Wilde. Did I hear her right?

"There's a different design every year," she said. "I think you could do a great job. If you want, I'll speak to the organizer—"

"Yes!" I said. I didn't even have to think about it! My own drawing, on posters! On T-shirts!

Coach Wilde looked pleased. "Wonderful," she said. "I'm so glad we found a way for you to participate, even if you can't run with us."

Then, blowing her whistle, she returned to the field. *Wheeeeeeeeeeeeeeeeeet!*

I was all by myself again. Suddenly, I realized that drawing the Wonder Run poster wasn't going to be enough. I wanted to be out there, running with everybody else.

The minute practice ended, I wobbled over to Coach Wilde. I didn't even say hi. "I was thinking about what you said," I began.

"About the drawing?" she asked. "I can get you all the specific information you'll need—"

I shook my head. "No. About not running in the Wonder Run," I said. "I *want* to run. And my toes should be healed pretty soon, in a week or two. Not more than two weeks."

Coach smiled sympathetically. "I'd love it if you could run with us," she said. "But you have to train for a 5K, Abby. It takes consistent effort to get your body ready for a race like that. All the things we're working on—speed, strength, and endurance—don't happen overnight. They happen over time."

"So—it's too late?" I asked. "There isn't anything I can do?"

Coach Wilde was quiet for a long moment, staring at me. "We could think about adding an extra coaching session every week," she said thoughtfully. "Maybe on Saturday mornings . . ."

"Yes. Definitely," I said. "I will be there!"

"Let's talk to your parents first," Coach Wilde said. "If they're on board, so am I."

A few days later there was a surprise when I got to school. Mr. Smiley had pushed our desks together into groups of four.

"At every group, you'll find a blank map of the United States," he said. "It's your job to label each state correctly.

Don't forget that spelling and penmanship count. You may talk—quietly."

I didn't say it was a good surprise.

My group had Maya and Savannah and Elliott.

"I wish we could work on our own maps, instead," Maya said, sounding worried. "I've already had to start my rough draft over *twice*. I'm so bad at scale."

"I can help you with that," I said.

Maya flashed me a grateful smile. "Really?" she asked.

"Of course. I learned about scale in this art class I took last year," I replied. "There are—"

"Okay, guys, enough chatting," Savannah said importantly, pushing the paper over to Maya. "Let's get this done."

I mean, it made sense that Savannah gave the paper to Maya, who has the nicest handwriting of anybody, ever. But shouldn't she have asked first?

Just as I thought that, Maya glanced over at me and we shared a *look*; she clearly agreed with me, even though I hadn't said a word. I tried to hide my smile. It was the same kind of look that Zoe and I must've given each other about a billion times.

I spotted North Carolina first, and then glanced all the way across the country to California. It was such a big state! Even the name was fancy and glamorous. No doubt Zoe fit right in.

Savannah reached across the table and tapped the paper with the feathery topper on her pink pencil. "That's New York," she said, pointing at a state that was basically opposite of California. "My grandmother lives in the city, and we get to visit her every Christmas and do all the awesome Christmas stuff."

"Really?" asked Elliott. "That's so cool."

"It is," Savannah said. "It's *amazing.*"

Then she reached farther across the table to tap another state. She was saying something, but I wasn't paying attention to that, because the shoulder of her sweater had slipped a little, and now everyone could see it—the satiny pink stripe of her bra strap. I looked away fast, but when I glanced back, her sweater was still like that. She hadn't fixed it. Maybe she hadn't even noticed.

I had to tell her. She'd be so embarrassed, but I had to do it. I mean, anyone could see it! Even Elliott!

I carefully, quietly tore off a tiny piece of notebook paper and wrote in the itty-bittiest letters: "Your bra is showing."

Then I leaned over and dropped it in front of her. Savannah looked a little interested in my note . . . until she read it. Then she sighed, crumpled it up, and shrugged like she didn't even care. "So what?" she mouthed.

Now I was the embarrassed one, because I realized that maybe Savannah knew all along. Maybe she didn't care if everybody saw her bra strap.

Maybe she wanted them to see!

I looked around the room. There were sixteen girls in my class, including me. How many were wearing bras right now? Bras were supposed to be a big secret, just like underpants. I didn't think Savannah would be so eager for everyone to see the waistband of her underpants, but maybe I was wrong about that, too. I couldn't stop wondering about it. Did that make me weird? Would no one want to be my friend if they knew that right now, my brain was basically *Bras-bras-bras-maps-bras-bras-bras*?

My chest wasn't completely flat anymore. There was this teeny, tiny roundness under my nipples that was totally visible now. I mean, not when I had a sweatshirt on. But I knew what was coming next. It might take a while, but my breasts were going to keep growing. So I'd need a bra eventually. Maybe I already needed one, and I didn't even know it! How did you know if you needed a bra? It seemed like there should be some kind of sign or signal or something.

There was only one thing to do. I'd have to talk to Mom.

❋   ❋   ❋

I waited until Max was asleep. Then I found Mom in the kitchen, typetty-typing on her laptop.

"Mom," I said. "Are you busy?"

"Mm-hmm," she said, staring at the screen. "I have about fifty emails to answer."

I frowned, not that she noticed. She *never* noticed, not anymore. I'd have to try something else. Then I remembered what Dr. Camfield said.

"I am trying to keep the lines of communication open," I told her.

Those were the magic words.

"Oh. Of course," she said, standing up fast and grabbing her cell. Neither one of us did any talking as we walked to my room. When the door was closed so that nobody could hear, I took a deep breath and said it.

"I think I'm ready for a bra."

"A bra?" Mom repeated.

"Other girls in my class are wearing them," I said. This was probably a dumb thing to say, but it was the first thing that popped into my mind.

"Okay," Mom said. "Yes. A bra. If you want one. I mean, if you're ready. On Saturday we'll go shopping and have you measured and—"

"What?" I squawked. "Measured?!"

"For a bra," Mom said. "To find out what size you need."

"How does that work?" I asked. I pictured the metal plate with the slide-y thing at the shoe store, where my feet got measured for new shoes. Did they have one of those for breasts? If they did, was it like some kind of torture device?

Did it *hurt*?

My chest wasn't sore, exactly. Well, sometimes it was. But mostly it was tender. Like all the time, in the back of my mind, I knew my brand-new breasts were there, and if for some reason I forgot and flopped down on my stomach or pressed my notebook against my chest, then they reminded me *fast* (yowch!).

"Don't look so alarmed," Mom said, laughing a little. "It's very discreet. The saleswoman will take you into a fitting room, and she'll use a tape measure to—"

I folded my arms across my body and shook my head. "Uh-uh. No way." If Mom thought I was going to let some total stranger wrap a tape measure around my chest, she didn't know me at all.

"All right," Mom said. "Would you . . . be more comfortable if *I* measured you instead?"

"You know how to do that?" I asked.

She nodded. "I'll have to refresh my memory, but I'm sure there are instructions online," she began. "I used to measure myself all the time in high school, hoping that my chest was getting bigger. Wishful thinking!"

Then Mom looked at me fast and cleared her throat. "There was so much focus on what a 'perfect' body should look like. I didn't understand then that bodies come in all shapes and sizes, and that's normal. Completely and totally normal! It's great, actually!"

"I know, I know," I muttered. We'd had this conversation once or twice or a trillion times before.

Mom was already staring at her phone again. "Here we go," she said. "Let me get a tape measure. I'll be right back."

Mom left her cell phone on my desk, so I stole a glance at the screen. There were these drawings—diagrams, I guess—of a lady with breasts and no head. Creeeepy! A tape measure was draped around her chest and—

Ping!

It was a text. I knew I shouldn't read it—I *knew* I shouldn't read it—but it was from Aunt Rachel, so how could I resist?

> Did Abby get a letter yet? I keep reminding
> Zoe to write to her

I dropped the phone back on the desk like it was a tarantula about to bite me. It was bad enough I knew Zoe hadn't written to me. But the thought that it was a *thing*—that Mom and Aunt Rachel knew, too, and were texting about it behind my back—made me want to shrink into an itty-bitty speck of dust that no one could see. That's how embarrassed I was. Imagine, Aunt Rachel telling Zoe to write to me, reminding her like it was just another chore—Don't forget to make your bed and write to Abby!

Mom came in with the tape measure. I tried to smile, and I guess she thought I was embarrassed about the measuring stuff because she was, like, almost professional about it. First, she wrapped the measuring tape around my chest under my armpits, which made me glad I had remembered to put on my deodorant that morning.

"This is how we measure the band size," Mom said.

Then Mom wrapped the tape measure around the swollen area, the biggest part of my breasts. I mean, not that any part of it was *that* big.

"And that's how we measure the bust size," she said.

"Bust?" I asked.

"It means breasts," Mom said. "It's kind of an old-fashioned word."

And a silly one, I thought. Bust. Breasts. Breastesesssss. Breast buds, like they were BFFs. And those were just the real words! The slang ones, the ones Mom would be mad if I said out loud, sounded even sillier.

I had to admit I was kind of interested in the numbers, so I stretched my neck to get a look. But Mom had already punched them into the website on her phone. Who knew there was a special kind of calculator all about bras? Was there an app, even? Did Zoe have it on *her* phone?

Mom was staring at the screen when her phone pinged with another text. Was it Aunt Rachel again? Or Mr. Taylor? Was she still working on my bra size? There wasn't much point in asking. It was obvious she was focusing on her messages. I started squirming around, wondering what else Mom and Aunt Rachel talked about in their texts . . . and wondering if Zoe knew they were talking about us, too. It was so incredibly unfair that our parents could text about us behind our backs. And I still wasn't even allowed to have a phone!

At last, Mom looked up from her messages. "Okay," she finally said. "This weekend we'll go to the mall. Promise."

CHAPTER 9

Saturday was a big day. I got to wear regular shoes for the first time in weeks. Goodbye, boot! Mom and Dad said that I couldn't toss my boot in the Halloween bonfire, so I did the next best thing and shoved it into the back of my closet, a graveyard for all the stuff I never want to see again.

Maybe even more important, Mom didn't have to go to work that morning. Instead, she took me to the mall so we could shop for bras. *Bras!!!* Somehow I was kind of dreading it and kind of excited at the same time. I tried to focus less on the shopping-for-bras part and more on the hanging-out-just-Mom-and-me part.

Halloween hadn't even happened yet, but the mall was ready for Christmas. Everything was decorated with loops of garlands and big shiny baubles. I was wearing my dangly jack-o'-lantern earrings, which made me feel pretty dumb when the speakers were playing Christmas carols.

But if I thought I felt out of place because of my Halloween earrings, that was nothing compared to how I felt in the bra department. We were suddenly surrounded by bras. Hundreds of bras. Maybe *thousands* of bras! Bras in every color, giant bras, tiny bras, bras with straps and bras with no straps and bras with convertible straps. There were bras made of plain cotton, like my underpants, and silky bras and lacy bras, and bras with beads and bras with bows. And padded bras that stuck out all by themselves, and push-up bras, and bras with curved wires hidden inside them.

Where would we begin?

Mom scanned the racks, looking for something; I don't even know what. Then this lady glided toward us. I couldn't tell you what she looked like. All I could see was the tape measure hanging around her neck, swinging back and forth.

"Can I help you?" she asked.

"No!" I yelped, staring at the tape measure.

Mom shot me a look and turned to the lady with a smile. "Can you point us in the direction of the training bras?" she asked.

137

Training bras? Training for what, exactly? An image of Coach Wilde flashed into my head, yammering about training. It was almost like I could hear her voice ringing in my ears.

No, wait. I really could hear her voice.

"So you're saying *all* these bras are buy one, get one free?"

Oh no, I thought. *No, no, no, no, no.* There was no way—NO WAY!—that Coach Wilde was at the same store, at the same time, in the same department, as me. And buying bras. Bras! *Whyyyyy?!*

I went into stealth mode to hide. I shrunk down to make myself shorter and took a few steps backward.

Thunk!

That was the back of my head, cracking into a rack. "Ouch!" I yelped. So much for stealth mode. But it was even worse because the rack was crammed with those slinky, slippery bras, and the next thing I knew, there was a bra avalanche. A bravalanche!

"Abby!" Mom said. Why was she being so loud? Didn't she get the stealth-mode memo? "What's going on? Did you hurt yourself? Is it your toes?"

"No," I whispered, rubbing the bump on the back of my head. "I'm fine. Let's go—"

"Why are all these bras on the floor?" Mom asked, frowning. "What happened?"

"I know! I'm picking them up!" I cried. But those bras were more slippery than a seal. It was like they *wanted* to fall onto the floor.

Then the saleslady was hovering, "oh dear"—ing all over the place, and somehow, despite being in *total stealth mode*, I had attracted a crowd. In the bra department!

"Abby?"

Coach Wilde's voice was unmistakable. There she was, looming over the racks with a giant stack of giant bras under her arm.

"That's quite a pileup," she cracked, staring at my bra mess. Then she knelt down, scooped a bunch of bras into her arms, and slapped them onto the rack like it was no big deal.

For her, those dumb bras stayed put.

"How's the foot?" Coach Wilde asked.

I stretched out my foot and wiggled my toes. Without the buddy tape, they felt so free! "All better," I said. "I can start running again on Monday."

"That's great news!" she said. Then she turned to Mom. "I don't know if you're in need, but I've gotta tell you, these are the best sports bras I've ever tried, and they're on sale. Buy one, get one free!"

"Really?" Mom said, sounding way too interested.

Oh, please, I thought. The last time Mom exercised was never. Why would she need two sports bras? She didn't even need one.

"They're not kidding about the moisture wicking," Coach was saying. "You can sweat a gallon in one of those puppies and never feel a thing."

I did not know it was possible for words to kill you, but I was pretty sure I was going to fall over and die if Coach Wilde said one more thing about *moisture* or *sweat*. And why did she bring puppies into it? Why was Mom following her over to the sports bras? Why, why, why, why!

"Another tip: They run small. Snug is good; you want the support, but you don't want to squash your girls," Coach Wilde was telling Mom. They didn't even notice that I was dead from embarrassment. "So I'd advise you to size up."

"What's the smallest size?" Mom asked. "I wonder if we could get some for Abby."

"Well, sure! I've sent several young runners to try the junior line," Coach said.

Mom picked up a snazzy-looking bra with a bunch of neon triangles, isosceles and scalene and—*Argh*, why did that bra make me think about Mr. Smiley's math lesson? *What* is *wrong* with my brain?—and she even held it up to my chest right there in the middle of the store, in front of Coach Wilde and everybody.

I batted her hand away. I think she got the message.

"You can try some on in the fitting room," Mom said quickly. "We'll get, ah, a variety of sizes."

"They run small," Coach Wilde said again, trying to be helpful.

"Thanks so much," Mom said, sounding like she really meant it.

I grabbed the stack of bras from Mom's hands and zoomed off to the fitting room, where I ducked into one of the dressing rooms like it was a secret hideout where no one would ever find me. There was a giant mirror, taller than me, and I saw right away that my whole face was red-hot and blazing. I closed my eyes and leaned forward, pressing my cheek against the mirror. It felt so good—silvery cold,

141

like ice on my fiery face. I could stand there for minutes, for hours, but then—

Knock-knock-knock!

I froze. What if it was that saleslady? What if it was Coach Wilde?!

"Need any help?" Mom's voice, low and soft, came through the door.

"Uh . . . no. Not yet," I replied. Then I peeled my face off the mirror, leaving a cloudy, oily patch behind. Ewww! I tried to wipe it off with my sleeve, but that just made it more smeary.

I shrugged out of my shirt and stood there, staring at the first bra. I couldn't tell which side was the front and which side was the back. *Nope,* I thought.

So I reached for the second bra. This one had really pretty, lacy straps, and it was totally obvious which side was the front. Plus, the back had these tiny hooks. At least this one I would know how to put on.

Or so I thought.

I stuck my arms through the straps and stared at myself in the mirror. I looked like me but not me. Me, but grown up from the neck down—the kind of person who would wear a bra with lacy straps. From the neck up, though, I was still regular me. Red cheeks, oily nose, and Halloween earrings.

I twisted my arms around to attach the clasps. What a disaster! Every time I moved, the bra acted like it was trying to escape. Those little hooks were not having it. I was grunting and twisting until I looked like a pretzel. I wobbled a little and fell against the wall with a crash.

"Ow!" I yelped. My elbow throbbed, sending pain shooting up and down my arm. Why do they call it a funny bone when there is *nothing* funny about how bad it hurts?

"Abby!" Mom called again. She rattled the doorknob. "Can I please come in?"

I shut my eyes, trying to wish myself anywhere else. What kind of a loser can't even try on a bra without causing a catastrophe?

"Sure," I whispered.

Mom slipped in fast and shut the door behind her. I think she figured everything out without me having to tell her. "Let me teach you a trick," she said. Then Mom wrapped the bra around my waist with the breast part in the back. For half a second I wondered if *Mom* even knew how to put on a bra . . . until she showed me how to do the

143

clasps in the front, where I could *see* them, and then twist the fastened bra around so the clasps were at the back.

"Then you put your arms in the straps and lean over so your . . . breasts . . . fall into the bra," she explained.

Well. That made it about a thousand times easier.

It turned out Mom knew lots of secret tricks for putting on bras. With her help I was able to try on each of them, and eventually, we bought three: the lacy-strapped one, a convertible one, and a sports bra, too. But *not* the one with the triangles. I liked the one with stars much better.

As we left the store, I folded the top of the bag over and kind of hid it under my arm. It's not like the bag was see-through, but I definitely did *not* want anyone to know what was inside it.

"Phew," Mom said. "Bra shopping always makes me hungry."

"Really?" I asked, scrunching up my nose.

Mom burst out laughing. "I'm kidding!" she exclaimed. "But I could go for a cookie. How about you?"

"You know it!" I said. The fresh-cookie store in the mall was my favorite place to get a treat. Did Mom remember that?

I had a feeling that she did.

CHAPTER
10

I spent the entire weekend working on the Wonder Run design, which was not easy with Max constantly slinking into my room like I wouldn't even notice. I sketched it with pencil and then traced over it with black ink, and then I colored it in with my best markers, the ones I only use for really special projects. I even snuck out of bed on Sunday night to add a couple finishing touches. I couldn't help myself!

I knew Monday was going to be awesome before I even got out of bed. Not only did I get to wear *two matching shoes* to school, but in the afternoon I'd be back at Run Wild!— not just on the bench, but on the field! *And* I could show Coach Wilde and the whole crew my drawing. I almost skipped across the field after school, but the flutteries in my stomach kept me walking. I mean, I loved my drawing . . . but what if nobody else did?

"Look who's back in action!" Coach Wilde called when she spotted me. I grinned, and then I grinned even bigger when all the runners started clapping and cheering for me. For me! As if I wasn't one of the slowest, clumsiest runners in the group. But nobody seemed to care about that . . . so maybe I didn't need to care about it, either.

"I have something," I said. Then I searched my backpack for the special heavy-duty folder that had my artwork. I didn't want it to get wrinkled or creased or anything.

"Is this what I think it is?" Coach Wilde asked.

I nodded as I handed her the folder.

Everyone crowded around to see as Coach Wilde pulled out my drawing. I'd drawn a tiny house that looked like the pictures Mom showed me on her phone, except in my drawing, it was made out of gingerbread. It had bright little gumdrops and swirly peppermints, with a warm, happy light shining in the window, and snowflakes drifting outside. And the best part, my favorite part, was a lawn flamingo standing out front, wearing a Santa hat.

Then, in my best lettering, I wrote:

WONDER RUN
HOME FOR THE HOLIDAYS

There was a long quiet; long enough for me to start worrying. What if it was terrible, what if it was garbage, what if—

"Abby," Coach Wilde began. "This is perfect. Perfect!"

My cheeks hurt from how big I smiled.

"It's going to look so great on the T-shirts and the posters and the flyers and in the newspaper—"

"The newspaper?" one of the boys asked.

Coach Wilde nodded. "The Wonder Run is a big deal. You'll see! And right now, I want to see all of you doing your best push-ups. Let's go for . . . twenty!"

Twenty?!

As if she could read my mind, Coach Wilde looked over at me. "Ten for you, Abby," she said. "We'll get you back up to speed, but don't push yourself too hard today, okay?"

"Okay," I promised. I'd do whatever Coach Wilde said. Because the Wonder Run was coming . . . and I wanted to be ready.

147

"Hey," Maya said, just before we dropped to the ground. "When the flyers are printed, do you want to go around and hand them out together?"

"Sure," I said. "Definitely. You could—you could come over to my house after practice sometime."

"Can't wait!" Maya said.

Who would have ever thought I'd be grinning during push-ups?

Only a week later, Coach showed up at practice with a ginormous stack of posters and flyers. And there it was—my drawing, right in the middle, flamingo and all! There were sign-up sheets, too, and forms where we could keep track of the donations we received. Maya and I took a bunch. We couldn't wait to tell the whole world about the Wonder Run.

After practice, Dad drove us back to our house. He let us have ice cream for a snack, and I can tell you, that is something Mom would never do. She would have given us apples. Or maybe bananas.

Maya and I were in a big hurry to start handing out flyers. We both slurped up our ice cream superfast. It was nice to hang out with somebody who could eat ice cream as quickly as me.

"Make sure you're back before it gets dark," Dad said, glancing out the window. It was getting dark earlier and earlier, but if we hurried, I figured we could stop by every house on my street. And maybe more!

At the first house, Maya and I stood on the doorstep. "You can ring the doorbell," I told her.

"No, you do it," she replied, nudging my arm. "They're your neighbors."

That's when I realized that we were both kind of nervous. So I took a deep breath, rang the doorbell, and waited. Mrs. Horowitz answered.

"Oh, hi, Abby," she said.

"Hi, Mrs. Horowitz," I said. "I wanted to tell you about the Wonder Run. It's on December twenty-second, and we're going to raise money for a new tiny-house village."

I handed her a flyer.

"I read about this in the paper," she said. "It's a great idea."

That was a good sign! I looked over at Maya, and she nodded encouragingly, so I said, "You can help by running with us, or sponsoring a runner."

Mrs. Horowitz laughed. "Thanks, but I'm not really up for running a 5K," she said. "Are you running, Abby?"

"Yup," I said. "It's my first 5K ever."

"Well, in that case, I'd be delighted to sponsor you," she said.

And then she gave me a check for ten dollars! It was that easy!

Maya and I took turns after that. One house for me, one house for her. The sun was dipping down behind the bare trees, and even wearing my coat, I shivered a tiny bit, but I didn't want to stop. Not just yet.

Across the street and down the block, though, was Zoe's house. Her old house. I could see a different car in the driveway, and lights on in the window, and my heart squeezed so hard, it hurt. I didn't want to see the new family who lived there or how they might have changed Zoe's house. I'd already seen more than I wanted.

"This way," I said, steering Maya around the corner. It was definitely close to dark. We only had time for one or two more houses. And then I realized—we were on the same street as the flamingo house.

"You've gotta see this," I told Maya. We skip-ran halfway

down the block, and when we got to the flamingo house, I held up my arm and said, "Ta-da!"

Since Halloween was over, Mrs. Flamingo had re-arranged the flamingos again. Now they were playing football, with jerseys and helmets, and a real football right in the middle of them. There were even a couple cheerleader flamingos with pink pom-poms!

Maya burst out laughing. "That's the dumbest thing I've ever seen," she said. "My mom says lawn ornaments are so tacky."

I didn't say anything for a moment. *Zoe* never would've called the flamingo house dumb or tacky. It just showed that even though Maya was becoming an awesome friend, she couldn't take Zoe's place.

Nobody could.

"I like them," I said. "Mrs. Flamingo puts them in funny poses every month. That's why I drew one on the poster."

Maya looked embarrassed. "I didn't mean—Is her name really Mrs. Flamingo?"

"No," I said. Before I could say anything else, a car pulled into Mrs. Flamingo's driveway. I recognized that rusty, dent-y old car.

It belonged to Daphne.

It was still light enough that I could see her car was packed, just like it was when Dad and I delivered that package. Maya and I weren't doing anything wrong, but I still felt like we'd gotten caught.

Daphne got out of her car. "Hey," she said. "What's up?"

Her hair was extra short, with bright blue at the tips, and she had a bunch of shiny silver rings in her ears, and even one in her nose. She smiled at us in a funny way that made me feel better.

"Visiting the flamingos?" she asked. "They have quite a fan club."

"They do?" I asked, surprised. For some reason I always thought only Zoe and I paid attention to them. But now I realized how silly that was.

"Sure," Daphne said. "One year my aunt was late switching them up, and she actually got an anonymous note about it."

"Seriously?" I asked.

"Seriously."

I wasn't sure what to do next. Knowing Daphne lived in her car, I wasn't about to ask her for a donation. But

Maya didn't know that, and before I could send her, like, a signal or anything, she was telling Daphne all about the Wonder Run.

"Tiny houses, huh?" Daphne said as Maya gave her a flyer. "I could use one of those."

"You don't live here?" Maya asked.

"Nah," Daphne said, glancing at the house behind her. "Don't get me wrong, I love my aunt and all, but . . ."

A long pause came next. It stretched on and on. I don't think Maya knew what to say next, and I *know* I didn't.

Daphne finally shrugged. "It's her house, but it's my life, you know?" she said.

I didn't really know, but I nodded, anyway. There were so many things I wanted to ask Daphne, like *What's it like living in your car?* and *Is it comfy?* and *Do you get cold?* and *Would you live in a tiny house, really, if you could?*

"Hey," Daphne said, looking closer at the flyer. "Is that a flamingo in a Santa hat?"

"Yeah," I admitted. "You can add me to the flamingo fan club. I was . . . inspired by them."

"Aunt Ava's gonna love that," Daphne said. "Can I have an extra flyer for her?"

"Sure," I replied. As I gave her one, Daphne pressed a couple crumpled-up dollars in my hand.

"It's a really cool thing you're doing," she said. "It's going to help a lot of people."

"You could run in the 5K, too, if you want," Maya told her.

"Maybe I will," Daphne replied.

"We've gotta go," I said. "It's getting dark. My dad will be mad."

"I know what that's like," Daphne said, with that funny little smile again. "It was nice to meet you. Come back and visit the flamingos anytime."

Then, as Maya and I started walking back to my house, Daphne went back to her car. Maya started talking about our map project, which was good, because I didn't want to talk about Daphne and the rusty car where she lived.

But I did hope that Daphne would run with us.

❀ ❀ ❀

The next day I got the rough draft of my map back from Mr. Smiley—and he gave me an A! I was so excited. We had one month—November—to create the final map, and I knew I needed to get started right away.

But when I got home from school, I decided to write to Zoe first. I wanted to tell her all about meeting Daphne, and the flamingo fan club, and how my Wonder Run drawing was going to be *everywhere*. I sat down at my desk and pulled open the drawer to get my flamingo stationery.

I blinked a few times. It took me a second to realize what had happened.

Max.

Max had happened.

Max in my room, Max with crayons and pencils and my best markers, Max writing his name on each and every piece of my special flamingo paper.

"Max!" I thought I was going to yell, but the word sounded more like a scream-howl. The kind of sound that would make any adult in the building come running at top speed.

And Mom did. "Abby! What's wrong? Are you okay?" she asked, breathless.

Max wandered into my room at the same time, like it was no big deal, like he hadn't done anything wrong. I wanted to pummel him, but I just clenched my hands into tight fists for a second.

Then I picked up the whole stack of flamingo paper and threw it at him!

Flamingos flying at last, I thought as the pages fluttered throughout my room. But Max was *laughing,* like it was all some big joke, like he hadn't *ruined* all my flamingo stationery!

"Abby!" Mom exclaimed. "What's going on?"

I flung out my hand and pointed at Max. "*He* wrote his name on every page of my flamingo stationery!" I yelled. "Every single page!"

You would think Mom would understand how bad it was that Max did this. But no. Her eyes got all wide, and she grabbed a piece of paper from the floor. "Max!" she said. "You wrote your name!"

"Uh-yup," Max said. "I learneded it at Little Learners."

"This is incredible!" Mom exclaimed.

That only made me madder. First of all, it was not incredible. His *M*s were a mess, like a craggy mountain range. His *A*s looked like *Q*s. And some of his *X*s were so big, they took over the whole page.

And second—

"This was *my* stuff," I said, practically shaking. "He had *no* right to come in here and write on *my* paper and ruin it! He ruined all of it! Like he ruins everything! Like he ruins my whole life!"

I regretted saying that even before I saw the way Max was looking at me, his face kind of wobbly and scrunchy, like he was trying not to cry. I mean, it *was* true. Sort of true. Well, not really true at all.

Mom's face was scrunched up, too, but in a mad way. "Max, go watch your show," she said.

"Sorry I ruined your life, Abby," he said as he slunk out the door.

That made me feel even worse.

Then it was just Mom and me, alone, surrounded by flamingo papers with Max's name all over them.

"Abby," Mom began. "Do you know why Max wrote all over the flamingo papers?"

"Because he hates me and wants to wreck my stuff."

Mom shook her head. "No. Not at all," she said. "Because he looks up to you and wants to be just like you. Look how much you inspire him. He's seen you writing on

157

the flamingo paper so many times that he tried to do the same thing."

I hadn't thought of it like that before. Could Mom be right? Was that why Max was always getting into my stuff? Did he really want to be like me?

"He'll learn to leave your stuff alone," Mom said. "He's still learning, every day. But we don't have to break his spirit to teach him. Writing his name for the first time is something we should celebrate. Not make him feel ashamed about."

I didn't say anything. How come *Max* had done something bad, but I was the one getting lectured? Part of me wanted to get even madder. But the deeper, truer part knew Mom was right. And that just made me sink further into a pool of miserableness.

Mom could tell, of course. She wrapped her arm around my shoulders and gave me a squeeze. "I have an idea," she said. "Let's call Zoe."

I shrugged and stared at the floor. "She never answers." *Or calls me back,* I thought—but I kept that part to myself.

"Let's try, anyway," Mom said, holding out her phone. "It's three hours earlier there. I bet she's home from school by now."

My feet started tapping while I waited for Zoe to answer. The phone rang . . . and rang . . . and rang . . .

"Hey, this is Zoe! Leave me a message or, even better, just send me a text! Bye!"

I didn't do either. And I didn't say anything as I gave back Mom's phone.

"Listen. I have another idea," she said. "We can order more stationery. I can place the order right now and have Daddy pick it up on his way home."

"Don't bother," I said. The way my voice sounded surprised even me—not just mad or sad, but both combined, and maybe even a little hopeless, too. The truth was that I already knew I didn't need more flamingo stationery. What was the point? Zoe had never written back to me, not even once. It was clear she was never, ever going to.

I folded my arms over my stomach and curled into myself.

"Hey," Mom said. "This seems bigger than your stationery. What's up? You want to talk about it?"

"No," I said into my arms. "I want to be alone."

Mom paused. Then she sighed and said, "Okay."

Just like that, she was gone.

Mom used to always know what I was thinking and what I needed. But not anymore. Just because I told her to go away didn't mean I wanted her to do that. Just because I said I wanted to be alone didn't mean that I really did.

After a few minutes I decided that I needed to write to Zoe after all. Just one last time. I got out a plain white piece of paper and sat at my desk.

Hey Zoe.

I always have so much I want to tell you, every day. That's why I have been writing to you so much. But I never thought that maybe you don't need to hear every little thing. What's going on with you? I have no idea, because it's been such a long time since we talked. And you never wrote to me—

I stopped and crossed out that last part. I didn't want to make her feel bad. I just had to tell the truth. It should've been the easiest thing in the world. And all of a sudden, it was.

I hope California is sunny and golden, every day. I hope you have so many friends, you can't remember all their

names. I hope you love school so much, you want to skip there every morning. I hope your new room is big and comfy and extra colorful now. I hope you are happy, all the time, about everything. I hope you know we miss you and love you lots here in North Carolina.

I hope we see each other again someday.

Love,

Abby

I put the plain paper in a plain envelope and stuck a plain stamp in the corner. This letter didn't need stickers or glitter pens or anything special. It was the last one I was going to write to Zoe—for a while, at least—and that made it special enough, all on its own.

My feet were still tapping. My room was like a cage. Suddenly, I realized what I wanted—no, *needed*. What would make me feel better than anything else.

I grabbed my running shoes.

"Mom!" I hollered as I zoomed to the kitchen. "Mom!"

She was already on her laptop. "What's up?" she said, still staring at the screen.

"Can I go for a run?" I asked, all in a rush.

That got her attention. "Now?" she said, glancing up. "By yourself?"

"Just around the block," I pleaded. "It's not dark yet. Please? I really feel like I want to go running."

I held my breath, waiting for her answer. Mom and Dad had never let me go around the neighborhood alone before . . . but I *was* almost ten.

"Okay," Mom finally said. "Just once. Watch for driveways and don't—"

"Thanks! Love you! Bye!" I exclaimed.

I burst out the door and started running before I even reached the sidewalk. My feet, crunching over dry brown leaves. My lungs, full of frosty autumn air. My heart, pounding harder, stronger, better.

Sunlight filtered through the bare branches, making the dark shadows of trees and buildings and even me streeeetch way long, but as I ran, I didn't feel like one of those shadows.

No. I felt like the sun itself—warm and shiny and glowing. And ready to light up the whole wide world.

CHAPTER
11

The days got shorter and shorter, but that didn't explain how they also passed by faster and faster. Life was a blur of Run Wild! practices and extra training sessions with Coach Wilde, and ringing doorbell after doorbell to get more donations before the deadline, and homework and so many maps that states and capitals and countries swam through my dreams.

It wasn't quite cold enough for snow, but it smelled like it. My cheeks were red and raw when I got home from the last round of door knocking in my neighborhood. I stared at my tally sheet, which was due tomorrow with all the donations I'd collected. I was still twenty-six dollars short of my goal. There was no one else to ask, either.

I wandered into the living room and flopped down onto the couch with a big sigh. It was loud enough that Max asked, "What?" without looking away from the TV.

"I wanted to raise more money for the Wonder Run," I said, staring at the ceiling. "But I didn't meet my goal. And there's nobody else to ask."

"You could ask me," Max replied.

Since Max was still staring at the TV, I could roll my eyes without him seeing. Please. As if Max had money. "Max, do you want to sponsor me for the Wonder Run?" I said automatically. "All the money we raise will go to building a tiny-house village for the homeless."

Max didn't answer. Obviously he was sucked into his show. He probably didn't even hear me.

A few moments later, though, I felt something cold and metal plunk off my forehead. Then it happened again!

"What the what?" I yelled as I scrambled up.

Max was standing at the end of the couch, holding Pet upside down. All those quarters, dimes, nickels, and pennies poured over the cushions and spilled onto the floor. It was a money waterfall!

"Max! Where'd you get all this money?" I exclaimed.

"Pet gets hungry a lot," he said, as if that explained it. "But I guess he ate too much money, and now he has to throw up. *Huuuueeegggggghhhhhh.*"

Grosssssss. Max's puking sounds were almost too real, but that didn't stop me from giving him the biggest, fiercest squeeze-hug ever. Then I showed him how to arrange the coins in dollar-size stacks: four quarters, ten dimes, twenty nickels, and—*eesh*—a hundred pennies.

Then, together, we counted by dollars.

"One, two, three, four," I began.

"Seventeen, fifteen, ninety-twelve," Max added.

I focused on the real numbers. Then I looked up at Max and grinned. "Max," I began. "You and Pet have saved thirty-seven dollars and twenty-four cents!"

"Is that a lot?" Max asked.

"It's enough to meet my goal and have eleven dollars and twenty-four cents left over for you," I said. "I mean, for Pet."

Max nodded seriously. "Pet's hungry again. Chomp, chomp, chomp!" he said.

"Chomp, chomp, chomp," I echoed as the money went *clink, clink, clink.* I couldn't wait to tell Maya and Mom and Coach Wilde that I'd met my fundraising goal.

I couldn't wait to tell everybody!

Then I heard the door open and close. Mom was home. I ran into the kitchen just as she dropped a stack of mail on the counter. "Hey, Mom, guess what?" I asked.

"Hmm?" Mom asked. She was already staring at her phone. She obviously wasn't looking at me—or even listening. I wished I could shake her arm, scream, do *anything* to get her attention.

Well, maybe I could—

Just then, something on the counter caught my eye. I recognized the purple envelope even before I saw my name written on it.

I didn't say another word. Instead, I zoomed right off to my room. I closed the door and stared at the letter. My letter. From Zoe.

At last!

Abby!

I am the worst. I'm so sorry. I owe you a million letters. I keep trying to write, but I don't know where to begin. I have too much to say. Even this letter is going to be kind of short because I think I need to just write this and send it. Ahhh. Eeeee. Okay. Here goes. My big secret . . .

I don't have bumps. I don't need deodorant. I definitely don't need a bra.

I spent a stupid lot of time worrying about it after I got your letters, so Mom took me to my new doctor, and she says I'm fine and everything's fine. She says I'm right on time for me, and you're right on time for you. I guess we all have our own time for this stuff. I feel dumb for worrying about this, but I feel . . . like, left out? That's my second secret. Even though I know you don't care that I haven't started changing at all, I'm still worried. What if I have, like, a baby body forever?

See? There I go again. Arrrrrggggggghhhh. Mom says it's not an easy time for anybody, and I guess she's right about that, at least.

I have one more secret, but I'm going to save that for later. Sorry! I know that's evil, but I can't help it. Ha-ha-ha-ha.

I miss you all the time. Thanks for writing to me so much. Getting a letter from you makes my whole day awesome, even if everything else about it was lousy.

Love,

Z

PS I hope you haven't been trying to call me. Mom took away my phone.

So that *is why she never tried to call me back!* I thought.

I read Zoe's letter again, and then I read it a third time. It had never even occurred to me that Zoe hadn't started puberty, too. She'd always been ahead of me in everything. But not this, I guess. I felt bad that I'd made her worry. And what was with all these secrets she kept mentioning? We'd never kept secrets from each other before.

I tried to focus on the good parts, like that Zoe missed me, too, and that she loved getting my letters. I decided right then and there that I would start writing to her again. But maybe I wouldn't write about the puberty stuff anymore.

At least, not until Zoe was experiencing it, too. I didn't want to make her worry even more.

I hid Zoe's letter under my bed and wandered back to the kitchen. "Guess what? I got a letter from Zoe!" I told Mom.

"Nice," she said, staring at her phone, swiping the screen.

Nice.

That's it.

I don't think she even heard what I'd said.

Maybe on a different day, I would've slunk off to my room and sulked in silence. But not today.

"Hey," I yelled. "Hey! I'm right here!"

Mom glanced up and frowned. "What's wrong, Abby?"

"Your stupid phone is what's wrong," I shot back. "I'm right here! But it's like I'm a ghost when you're on your phone. A ghost girl instead of a daughter. Is that what you want?"

Mom looked like I'd slapped her in the mouth.

"Here's what I don't get," I continued. "When we were at the doctor's, remember, you said, 'I thought we had more time,' and I keep wondering, more time for what? You staring at your stupid phone?

"I guess it's just another thing that's more important than me," I said. "Your texts are more important than me, and your laptop is more important than me, and your job is more important than me—"

And then something bizarre happened. I burst into tears. Big, salty, wet ones. I don't know who was more surprised, me or Mom.

"Oh, Abby," she said, rushing across the room and folding me into a hug. I kept my shoulders stiff, though, and I didn't hug her back.

"Nothing's more important to me than you and Max," Mom said. "Nothing, nothing, nothing."

I didn't move a muscle. "You won't let me have a phone, but you're always on yours," I said. "Constantly. I don't even think you hear me when I talk to you."

"I do, sweet pea," Mom said. "I do. And it's true, my phone's a big distraction. When Mr. Tucker texts, he expects an answer right away. I don't know how to balance it yet. I don't know that anybody does."

I still didn't hug her back.

"And . . . I really love my job," Mom said. "I didn't think I would, but I do. I love the work I do, and I love getting a paycheck so we don't have to worry about money so much. I love that we can sign you up for art class again and maybe even take a vacation next summer. That sounds pretty good, doesn't it?"

"I guess," I said. I wasn't convinced, though, and Mom could tell.

"Let's make a deal," she said. "I promise you that I'll try to be better about putting my phone away and giving you my full attention. Okay?"

"Okay," I said.

"And here's your part of the deal," Mom continued. "I need you to try to understand that sometimes I've *got* to answer a text or an email right away. It's not my choice, and it's also not my fault. It's just the way the world works right now."

"Well, it's dumb," I said.

"I don't disagree," Mom said, wiping my face, then kissing it. "Maybe we'll be able to fix it by the time you're a grown-up. And if not . . ."

"What?" I asked.

"Maybe *you'll* be able to fix it," Mom said, with one of her crinkle-smiles. "Look at how you're already changing the world, Abby. Daddy and I can't wait to see what you'll do next. We're so proud of how hard you've worked for the Wonder Run. Not just how much you've trained, but all the time you spent making the poster, collecting donations . . ."

That reminded me. "I made my goal," I said. "Max helped. Max . . . and Pet. They gave me the last donation I needed."

"Why am I not surprised?" Mom said, smiling even bigger. Then something shifted, a little, around her eyes, and her smile got kind of wobbly. "What I said that day—in Dr. Camfield's office . . . I thought I'd have more time with little Abby. You're growing up so much faster than I expected. And now it's like you're standing at the bridge that leads to adulthood—not just standing but starting to walk across it— and the truth is, I adore you so much, just the way you are. I love you with all my heart."

This time, when she hugged me, I hugged her back.

CHAPTER
→12←

Race day.

Race day!

I jumped out of bed and got dressed in the dark. From my sports bra to my sneakers, my special gear was all ready to go. I pulled on these awesome leggings with glittering snowflakes on them, and a long-sleeved silver shirt. On top of that I layered my official race shirt, the one with my very own drawing on it. I didn't want to brag, but it was my favorite shirt now, and I figured it would be forever.

It was dark o'clock when I wandered into the kitchen, where Mom was drinking coffee at the table.

"Good morning to my favorite wonder runner!" she said, immediately closing her laptop.

"Morning," I said. I don't know if my smile was more nervous than excited, but Mom suddenly got up and hugged me.

"So excited for you," she whispered near my hair. "You hungry?"

Mom held out a variety box of instant oatmeal so I could pick any flavor I wanted.

"And I made a toppings bar!" she said proudly.

"Yum!" I exclaimed as I stared at all the little bowls Mom had arranged on the counter. Dried cranberries, raisins, glazed pecans, brown sugar, cinnamon, nutmeg. I wanted to have them all!

When the oatmeal was ready, Mom handed the bowl to me. "Go to town," she said.

I fixed up the best bowl of oatmeal the world has ever seen and ate it up, every bite. Soon, there was a big commotion as Mom and Dad and Max got ready to go. For once, I didn't have to rush. I was ready. I'd been ready for ages.

We drove downtown, and what we saw there astonished me. It looked like the whole city had come to the race. There were racers wearing Santa hats, and racers wearing reindeer antlers. Racers with twinkling light necklaces. Racers with tinsel and curly ribbon hairbows. Racers with jingle bell wristbands that chimed whenever they moved. I spotted Mrs. Flamingo holding a big sign that said GO DAPHNE! so I figured Daphne must have decided to run in the 5K, too. I even saw Mr. Smiley and a little girl who must have been his daughter. They were wearing matching red tutus!

Most of all, though, was the joy. Laughter filled the air, swirling around us like snowflakes. There were lots and lots of people there, at least a thousand, and I'd never seen so many people who were so happy, all at the same time.

Dad drove over to the lot where everybody from Run Wild! would meet up. I could see Coach Wilde holding up a big sign, with tons of Wild Runners gathering around her.

"Good luck, Abby," Mom said, reaching over the seat to squeeze my hand. "We'll be waving at the halfway mark."

"And we'll see you at the finish line," Dad added.

"See you at the finish line," I replied, hoping I would make it there.

I reached over to mess up Max's hair for luck. He howled in outrage but was strapped into a car seat so he couldn't do anything. Then I got out of the car and hurried over to the group. Maya was waving really big so I could find her in the crowd. We'd already decided we were going to run together. That's because we weren't just running buddies. We were real ones.

We did some stretches and warm-ups right there in the parking lot. Then Coach Wilde yelled, "Huddle up, Wild Runners!"

We formed a circle, side by side, shoulder to shoulder, Lucy and Leah and Charlie and Maya. And me.

As Coach Wilde started to speak, we leaned in even more.

"You're ready," Coach Wilde told us, taking a moment to make eye contact with every single one of us. "You've trained hard, and you've earned this. Remember, I wouldn't have let you sign up if I didn't know you could finish the race. I believe in you. I believe in every single one of you."

Her words hung in the chilly air; we breathed them in, and it was like they became part of us.

"Arms out. Hands in," Coach Wilde announced.

We stuck our arms into the middle of the circle, and for a minute, all you could hear was the soft *slap-slap-slap-slap* of one hand slipping onto another.

"Now, how are you going to run?" Coach Wilde asked.

"WILD!" we all screamed at the top of our lungs as we raised our hands high into the air.

As a big group we walked over to the starting line. It was almost time for the race to begin . . . ready or not.

"What's that?" I asked, pointing at a pair of weird-shaped black tube-and-box thingies.

"Those are confetti cannons," Maya told me.

"Confetti *cannons*?" I asked, worried already. How loud would they be? Could you get hurt by confetti if a *cannon* shot it at you? I was all ready to come up with more worries when suddenly—

Boom!

Boom!

The confetti cannons exploded, so loud they rattled my bones. And the confetti! All colors—hundreds, thousands, maybe *millions* of pieces, fluttering and flittering, like snow that wasn't cold, like rain that wasn't wet, like the fluffy part of a dandelion scattering on the wind and flying off to Wish Land. The confetti landed on my hair, my shoulders, my sneakers, but only for a second, because my heart leaped up and my feet leaped forward. Just like that, me and Maya were running, running, running . . .

I could almost hear Coach Wilde. "Pace yourselves," she would say. I thought about *endurance* and how bad I wanted to finish the race, so I slowed down a little bit. Next to me, Maya did, too.

The sun was rising higher in the sky now, gold light spilling over everything. Somewhere on the sidelines, the frost on the grass was probably glittering as it turned into dew, but I couldn't think about that, not now. My breath puffed out in little clouds, and we passed the first mile marker like it was no big deal. I could feel that my feet were already in a good rhythm. As we ran down the middle of the street, it was like I had springs in my shoes, the way my feet would hit the ground and push me right back off, moving up and forward, forward, always forward—

We were each running on our own, but running brought us together. It made us one. That's how Maya could tell when I started having trouble. It wasn't a big thing. Probably not that easy to notice. But my feet got heavier—my steps were slower—instead of touching the ground and spiraling into the stratosphere, I felt like I was sinking into the pavement, like my shoes were scraping the cement. *Ratzit*, I thought. *I'm not going to finish.*

"Come on, Abby," she said. "You can do this! You know you can!"

"Uhhhh," I said, focusing on my breathing. My lungs felt so stretched out, like a gum bubble ready to burst.

"We're in this together," Maya said firmly. "You and me. Come on, we'll hit the halfway point and grab a water—"

"Halfway point?" I said in surprise. Had we gotten so far, so fast?

"Yeah—see it? We're getting closer every second," she said. "Let's do it!"

Maya was my running buddy. I couldn't let her down. Plus, Mom and Dad and Max would be at the halfway point. I didn't want to let them down, either. I pushed forward, thinking about one thing only: the next step. And that's how I ended up taking another step, and another, and another, until—

The halfway point! The volunteers held gleaming handbells that flashed as they swung back and forth. The clear, bright notes rang out through the frosty air, almost like a carol.

Then I spotted my family, just like they'd promised. Max was perched on Dad's shoulders. "Abby! Abby! Abby!" he hollered, shaking Pet high above his head. The money inside Pet clinked merrily, just like a bag of jingle bells.

"Go, Abby!" Dad yelled. "You can do it!"

"Abby!" Mom shrieked, so loud that I probably should have been embarrassed, but I'll be totally honest, I actually loved it. "Run wild, Abby! Run wild!"

I swung my arm out in a sideways wave as I passed. Then I got right back in my groove, arms and legs moving with the same goal, the same purpose. After we passed the second mile marker, the strangest thing happened. Things started to kind of fade away. I mean, I *knew* there were crowds on either side of the course, screaming and cheering and blowing air horns. I *knew* Maya was running right alongside me. But I was only really aware of my running.

In some burrow-y part of my brain, I thought I heard someone call my name. But that couldn't be right. My family had been back at the halfway point, which I had just passed a few seconds ago, or maybe it was an hour ago. I couldn't tell anymore; time was too slippery.

"Abby! Abby! Go, Abby!"

My head started to clear. That was *definitely* my name. I glanced from side to side and saw a giant pink flamingo, as tall as me.

That's it, I thought. *I've lost it. Running has made me as bonkers as Coach Wilde.*

But it wasn't a real flamingo, of course. It was a girl wearing a flamingo hoodie, her familiar face peeking out with a giant grin. I recognized that face. I'd know it anywhere.

Zoe!

No—maybe—yes!

It was her, really and truly, Zoe standing on the sidelines, shaking pink pom-poms and screaming my name. I caught a glimpse of Aunt Rachel and Uncle Craig behind her, and that's when I realized they must have come home for Christmas.

More than anything, I wanted to run over to Zoe and give her the biggest, longest, bestest hug—well, almost more than anything. Because just then, I caught sight of the finish line, and I couldn't wait to cross it. There'd be a chance to hug Zoe very soon, and hang out nonstop, and say all the things I'd been saving up to tell her since August.

But now—now was my chance to cross the finish line. To finish the race.

It wasn't a line, exactly, but a giant arc of balloons, with a steady swirl of confetti and streamers twirling through the air. The confetti glinted and gleamed, all silver and gold, and there was so much clapping, so much cheering . . .

Maya and I reached for each other's hands at the same time. We held on tight, our fingers squeezing like a hug, and I think an extra burst of *speed*, of *endurance*, of *strength* charged through both of us as we pounded under the archway and past the finish line.

I bent over with my hands on my knees, breathing hard and smiling harder. The metallic confetti landed all over me, but I didn't bother to brush it off. I liked shining as much on the outside as I was on the inside.

CHAPTER
13

"Abby! Abby! Abby!"

A bunch of different people were calling my name. I spun around, grinning, and saw Mom and Dad—Max was still on Dad's shoulders—and Aunt Rachel and Uncle Craig and—

Zoe.

She whooshed up to me in her flamingo hoodie, and in a flash, we were hugging and laughing and shrieking. I knew our parents were taking a ton of pics with their phones, and I didn't even care.

"You didn't tell me!" I yelled, laughing.

"It was my third secret!" Zoe was laughing, too, and pulled back for just a second before she crushed me in another hug. "So—are you surprised?"

"*So* surprised," I said. "The most surprised *ever.*"

I took a step back and looked at her for a long minute. Zoe wasn't as tall as I remembered, but then I realized something. *I* was taller than I remembered. Now, when we stood together, our eyes matched up just about perfectly. And that was pretty cool.

"We're staying for ten days. Ten!" Zoe was saying. "That means Christmas Eve and Christmas and New Year's Eve and New Year's Day and—"

"Hang on. Where are you staying?" I asked, remembering the new family who had moved into Zoe's old house.

"With you, of course," Zoe said. "Can you believe it? It will be the world's best sleepover! You still have that trundle bed, right?"

All I could do was grin. This was the best news! Zoe sleeping in my room, and Uncle Craig and Aunt Rachel in the guest room, for *ten whole days—*

That's when I realized that maybe it was okay we had that extra room and those extra beds, after all.

Maya was nearby, with her mom, so I grabbed Zoe's hand and pulled her over to them. "Maya! This is my cousin,

Zoe," I said. "She lives in California now. I didn't know she was coming!"

Then I turned to Zoe. "This is Maya," I said. I wanted to tell her more, how much stuff we had in common, and how we'd worked together on Mr. Smiley's map project, and how all those hours running together had turned us into real friends. Before I could, Mom and Dad swooped in for a hug. I didn't stiffen up or pull away or anything, even when Max started whomping on my head from his perch on Dad's shoulders. Being squashed in the middle of my family, with all their hugs and kisses and head whomps, was the rightest and best place in the whole wide world.

"I am so proud of you!" Mom kept saying, again and again.

"You were running like a real champ," Dad said. "Champ. Hmm. How does that sound to you?"

"I like it," I said. "I like it a lot, actually."

"I want to be a Wild Runner, too!" Max announced.

That reminded me of something I needed to do. I mean, someone I needed to see.

"Hang on," I told everyone. "I'll be right back."

It wasn't hard to find Coach Wilde. Her floofy, poofy ponytail stuck out above the crowd, as usual, and it was even easier to spot her with her tinsel scrunchie winking and glinting in the sunlight.

I bounded across the lot until I was standing next to her. "Coach," I said, a little out of breath. "Coach!"

Coach Wilde grinned. "Abby McAdams," she announced. "How does it feel to finish your very first 5K?"

"Incredible," I said. "Amazing. I never . . . I never thought I could do something like that."

"Well, I, for one, never had any doubts," Coach Wilde told me.

"I just wanted to say . . . thanks," I said. "Thanks for all the extra training and for believing I could do something I didn't even know I wanted to do. Thank you."

Coach Wilde just shrugged like it was no big thing. "That's what I'm here for," she said. "See you next session?"

"Definitely," I said firmly. It was maybe the easiest question I'd ever answered. I mean, *of course* I was going to sign up for Run Wild! again in January. There was no way I'd quit now.

When I got back to my family, everyone was talking about going out to breakfast. That's when I realized how hungry I was from all that running. It seemed like days since I made the world's best bowl of oatmeal early that morning. Maybe even weeks!

Not too far away, I saw Maya and her mom. And that gave me an idea. "Mom," I said, tugging on her coat. "Can we invite Maya, too?"

"I don't see why not," Mom said. "The more the merrier."

Maya was as hungry as I was, so we all decided to go. But first, Mom and Dad exchanged a glance. "You go ahead and get a table. Or a few tables," Mom said. "There's something I want to show Abby."

Another surprise? I wondered.

When I got into the car, I noticed that Max's car seat had already been moved to Aunt Rachel and Uncle Craig's rental car. So whatever Mom wanted to show me, she had planned it in advance.

We didn't say much as Mom drove through the city. Then Mom parked in front of a big old empty lot. There was some trash scattered over the cracked-up concrete, and even a few puny weeds poking through.

But there was also a silver chain-link fence around the lot, so shiny bright, I had a feeling it was new.

"Why—" I started to ask.

Mom pointed at a sign on the fence. Right away, I recognized my drawing of a gingerbread tiny house, Santa-hat flamingo and all. My heart was beating hard again, like I'd just finished the race.

I looked fast at Mom, who was smiling at me, her eyes watery-ish. I don't get why grown-ups cry when they're happy, but that's what she was about to do.

Then I read the sign.

FUTURE HOME OF WINSTON-SALEM'S

FIRST TINY-HOUSE COMMUNITY

COMING NEXT YEAR

"No," I said in kind of a whisper. "No way. Really? Is this real?"

"It's really real," Mom said. "Fifty tiny houses are going to be built right here. Construction starts in the spring."

I stared at the lot and didn't even see the trash or the weeds anymore. Instead, I used my imagination to picture neat rows of little houses, each one a different color, and flowers, and trees, and sidewalks, and hope.

"Fifty," I marveled.

Mom's hand reached for mine. "A lot of people have been working to make this happen," she continued. "And you're one of them, Abby. I just wanted to tell you how proud Daddy and I are. You saw a problem in the world, and you didn't turn away from it. Instead, you did everything you could to help fix it. That's not just impressive. It's inspiring."

"Thank you," I said.

"Thank *you*," Mom said. "We'll be back, for the ground breaking, and for the dedication ceremony. But now, let's go get some breakfast." ⸜

❋ ❋ ❋

When we got to The Breakfast Place, there was a big long table in the middle with my favorite people in the world. Best of all, Zoe and Maya had saved a seat for me, right between them.

"Abby!" Zoe said, waving.

I plunked down and grinned at them. "Did you guys order? I am so hungry," I said.

Zoe pushed the little basket of jam packets toward me. "Appetizer!" she said.

"Delicious," I said, slurping strawberry jam right out of the packet.

"I want to eat jam from a packet!" whined Max.

"Oops," I said, and Maya and Zoe cracked up.

"Abby, check it out," Maya said, pointing at a menu. "I'm getting the Wonder Run pancake special. It's three pancakes shaped like Christmas trees, and a whole cart of toppings so you can decorate them."

"Super yum," I said, licking my lips. "Make it two orders."

"Make it three!" Zoe added. "I saw the cart when I went to the bathroom, and it has M&Ms and gumdrops and blueberries and shredded coconut, which actually I hate because it kind of gets stuck in my throat when I eat it . . ."

"Me too!" Maya said, giggling. "It must be what it feels like to be a cat with a hairball."

"Do you have a cat?" Zoe asked. "I've always wanted one, but my dad's allergic."

"I do have a cat! Her name is Marigold! You could come over and meet her sometime. If you want," Maya replied, glancing at Zoe, then me.

"Really?" Zoe gasped. "I'd love to!"

"Me too," I said.

"I got Marigold when she was a tiny kitten who could fit in the palm of my hand," Maya told us. "We had to feed her from a little bottle."

"Awww!" Zoe cooed.

My smile stretched even bigger. Maya and Zoe were getting along really great. Maybe Maya's mom would let her sleep over one night during the break, before Zoe had to go back to California.

At the other end of the table, Dad and Uncle Craig and Aunt Rachel were laughing really hard at something. Mom and Maya's mom were talking together. Nobody was paying attention to Max. He looked pretty bored, sipping his orange juice through a paper straw, so I caught his eye and pretended to brush my hair with my fork. That made him laugh so hard that orange juice splurted out of his nose! Ratzit!

I quickly dropped my fork back on the table while Mom and Dad hurried to clean up Max. My place mat had a map of Winston-Salem on it—not a complete map, but most of downtown, and some of the neighborhoods around it. I could start where my house would be and trace my finger over to the flamingo house . . . then to the site of the tiny-house community . . . back to the restaurant . . . and then along the whole course for the Wonder Run. It was only a map on a place mat, and it probably wasn't even to scale, but I still couldn't believe I'd run that whole thing, all five kilometers.

But it was true: I could run a 5K. I could run the Wonder Run, all the way from start to finish. And if I could do that—me, who used to hate running, who fell over my own feet—then I could run in the Boston Marathon. I could run across the Golden Gate Bridge. I could run over the Rocky Mountains. I could run across the Mississippi River; I could run past the Great Lakes; I could run through New York City.

I could run anywhere.

And I could run anything!

ACKNOWLEDGMENTS

My agent, Jamie Weiss Chilton, has been an enthusiastic supporter of *Abby in Between* from the very start, and it's been a joy to explore Abby's journey with her. Thank you, Jamie, for believing in Abby—and in me.

I am so grateful for the keen and sensitive editorial guidance from Renee Kelly and Kaylee Hirzel-Duff, who helped me explore new avenues for telling Abby's story. The entire team at Penguin Workshop, including Mary Claire Cruz, Shara Hardeson, Kara Brammer, and Anna Elling, has my deepest appreciation for bringing their talents to my book.

My children's pediatricians, including Dr. M. Lynn Silkstone and Dr. Amy Yoder, have been compassionate and supportive beacons as our family has navigated all the stages of growing up. What I've learned from them over the years has informed the writing of this book. I'm also grateful to Coach Robyn Land McElwee and Coach Donnie Cowart for sharing their wisdom and expertise as they answered all my questions about running, especially how kids train to become stronger runners. Any errors in this book are mine alone.

It wouldn't be possible to write books without the encouragement and support of my family. My deepest gratitude to my husband, Dan, and our children, Clara, Sam, and Gabriel, who fill my days with love, laughter, and lots of inspiration. I adore you!

Finally, as I've been writing about Abby's experience with puberty, I've been honored by everyone who has trusted me with their own stories of growing up. While each puberty experience is unique and deeply personal, hearing about them from so many different people has underscored what is universal about this momentous and transformative time. I hope the publication of *Abby in Between* helps more people share their experiences. These stories—your stories—matter, and they deserve to be told.

HERE'S A SNEAK PEEK OF ABBY IN BETWEEN #2: FACE FORWARD

CHAPTER 1

"**T**ruth . . . or *dare!*"

I tried to make my voice sound dramatic and spooky, but all it did was make my friends crack up. I laughed, too, because honestly, it did sound pretty funny. So far, my New Year's Eve sleepover was completely amazing. We had already painted our nails and made jewelry out of about a zillion glow sticks. Truth or dare was going to take it to the next level. I'd spent the whole morning making a list of dares in my rainbow notebook, the one Mom and Dad had given me for Christmas.

And we were going to stay up until midnight and do the big countdown to the official start of the new year—my first time ever!

"Okay, okay, seriously." I tried again. "Truth . . . or—"

"Wait, wait, wait," Savannah interrupted me, holding up her hand. "Me first. I have one!"

And just like that, everybody turned to her. I don't know how Savannah always manages to get everybody's attention—and keep it, too.

"Maya," Savannah said to my best friend, "truth or dare?"

Maya took a deep breath. "Truth."

I held my breath a little, too. I didn't want Savannah to ask Maya something super personal or really embarrassing. But Maya is not the bravest. I don't think she's ever chosen "dare." Not even once.

A little smile flickered on Savannah's face. "Did you get your period yet?"

Ahhhh, I screamed inside my head. *She said it—she said it!*

Maya froze. She had the same look on her face as this raccoon we caught eating pizza out of the trash can outside last week: a mix of surprise and horror and alarm, like she sensed DANGER and was ready to run.

But Maya didn't run. She just shrugged and said, "Nope. Did you?"

"I didn't say 'truth,'" Savannah replied in this satisfied

way. "I don't have to answer anything."

"Ana Ramirez did," Grace spoke up. "I saw her with a pad in the bathroom before the break. She just, like, threw it in the trash, like no big deal. But I do *not* want to get mine for the fifth-grade campout. Did you know that bears can *smell* it?"

"Wait. Bears?" I said in alarm.

Maya, though, threw back her head and laughed. "Come on," she said. "My mom is a nurse at the hospital. I think we'd know if there were all these bear attacks on girls who have their period."

"I'm not going to risk it," Grace said. "If I have my period, I am *not* going."

"Well, I'm not going to miss it for anything," Maya announced. "Especially not for something like having my period. *If* I even have it by then."

"Hey," I said, tapping Maya's arm. "It's your turn, remember?"

"Right!" she said. Then Maya flashed me a grin and I just *knew* what was coming next. "Abby, truth or dare?"

With all that talk about periods and bears, I knew what I had to say. "Dare!" I crossed my fingers for luck. Hopefully, Maya would remember she's my best friend. Hopefully, she wouldn't tell me to do something awful.

"I dare youuuu . . . ," Maya began, "to . . . run outside . . ."

Savannah and Grace let out quiet screams.

"And touch the streetlight on the corner . . ."

More screams. Not so quiet this time.

"In your pajamas . . . with no coat and no shoes!"

Now I wanted to scream, too. Leave it to Maya to come up with such a good dare. And by good, I meant *terrible*. It had everything. Embarrassment! Who wants to go outside in their pajamas, where anybody could *see* them? Risk! If Mom caught me, I'd be in the biggest trouble ever. And also, this dare was going to be seriously uncomfortable. My toes were curling up just thinking about how cold the pavement would be.

Then I had a new thought. Maybe Maya had actually picked the perfect dare for me. After all, I'd gotten pretty fast at running since I joined the Run Wild! club last year. I thought I'd hate running more than anything, but I was wrong. Plus, Maya and I had become supergood friends, running together after school every day. I grinned. It was definitely not an accident that her dare for me included running.

"I accept this dare," I said in my most serious voice. "But first, I have to go to the bathroom."

"Sixty seconds," Savannah announced. "Otherwise, it counts as chickening out."

"Not chickening!" I retorted. A quick detour to my room on the way wasn't chickening . . . or cheating.

In my bedroom, I yanked on my bathrobe and pulled my old flamingo slippers out from under the bed. They were too small, but they'd be better than nothing.

When I left my room, all my friends were clustered by the front door, whispering so loud they might as well have been normal-talking.

"Shhh!" I hissed. If they got Mom's attention . . . or worse, woke up my little brother, Max . . .

Maya's face scrunched into a frown when she looked at me. "Hold up," she said. "My dare, my rules. And I said *no* shoes and *no* coat."

Now I was the one with the little smile. "A bathrobe isn't a coat," I replied. "And slippers aren't shoes. Like, you wouldn't wear them to school, right?"

Well, *everybody* had an opinion about that. Uh-oh. My sleepover was about to fall apart in the world's most boring circle meant anybody who looked out their window would see me in my jammies. *Nightmare!*

But it also meant that I was almost done with the dare. And almost back inside my warm, cozy house.

As I touched the freezing metal pole with the tip of my finger, a bright light flooded the street. My head jerked around and that's when I saw it: Dad's car, rumbling down the road.

Ratzit! Dad was almost home from work. I was about to be so busted!

Unless I could race him home . . . and win.

argument about whether slippers are more like shoes or socks. I had to do something . . . *anything* . . . to save it.

"Okay, *fine!*" I said, loud enough that everyone stopped talking. "No slippers. But I'm keeping the bathrobe."

"Okay," Maya agreed, nodding. "I'll allow it."

I kicked off my flamingos, unlocked the front door, and stepped outside.

The stars, sparkling like crystal through the cold, seemed so far away. When I shivered, it raced right into my heart and turned into a thrill of excitement . . . or maybe it was fear.

In the daytime, the corner wasn't far. Just five houses away. But at night?

It looked like a mile.

I shivered again. The longer it took, the worse it got.

Go, I told myself.

And just like that I was running down the path. It was so weird how the cold ground felt like fire on my bare feet. The grass, short and brown and sharp, wouldn't have been any better.

The streetlight cast a warm circle, a halo of light, and that was the best/worst part of this dare. Stepping into that